THE CHRISTMAS COTTAGE BY THE COVE

ELLEN JOY

For Jay. I love you. Thank you for my happily ever after.

Click HERE or visit ellenjoyauthor.com for more information about Ellen Joy's other books.

CHAPTER 1

Kate O'Neil didn't want to cry. Especially not in front of all the holiday travelers in line at the car rentals. The twenty-something behind the counter had no idea why Kate would be upset at being given a minivan, but she was. Because the last thing Kate wanted to drive after her fiancé dumped her was a family vehicle.

Instead of crying, she focused on how her chest tightened as though someone had wrapped a string of tinsel around it and pulled. She might be having a heart attack. She had the signs. It wasn't unheard of for someone in their thirties to have a heart attack was it?

The familiar heat rash crawled up her neck and perspiration curled the wisps along her forehead as tears stung her eyes. *Come on, Kate, pull it together.* She straightened and pushed back the minivan's keys, trying to keep her chin from trembling, but her words still came out wobbly. "But I reserved an SUV."

The girl looked blankly at her.

Kate's eyes darted toward the airport's window. The nor'easter that had threatened the flight up to the last minute made its predicted descent. At least a few inches had accumulated since baggage claim, and now large clumps of snow fell from the sky. She may have lived in Minnesota her whole life, but the Maine storm seemed more than she bargained for, especially in a minivan.

It wasn't the girl's fault, she reminded herself, taking in a deep breath, ignoring the irritated holiday travelers in line behind her. She had to keep it together, at least until she made it to her aunt's beach house, but her emotions had been as unpredictable as the storm. A tear teetered on the edge of her eyelid as a look of horror flashed across the girl's face.

She cleared her throat. "Are there any other rentals that have four-wheel drive?"

"You ordered an *all-wheel* drive vehicle."

Kate focused on her name tag instead of looking the girl in the face.

Brianna pointed to a screen that faced away from Kate. "Our minivan is the only one with all-wheel drive."

Brianna emphasized *all-wheel*, as though there was a big difference. Kate shook her head. "I'll take anything other than the minivan."

"But they won't come with all-wheel drive." The girl's face contorted in confusion. How could she explain that an eight-person vehicle was too much room for a woman who was alone for Christmas?

Brianna clicked the keys of her computer as Kate's hands tightened around the strap of her carry-on.

"You'll love the minivan," said a middle-aged woman behind her in line. "With the snow, an all-wheel drive vehicle is what you want for your family."

Kate unconsciously rubbed the band of her engagement ring with her thumb, but the habit made her throat ache and tears quivered once again in her eyes. With one last ditch effort, she resorted to begging. "Please, I'll take anything, *anything*, other than the minivan."

"Sorry, ma'am, but with the holidays, we only have the vehicle your family reserved."

"I don't have a family!" Her voice projected more than she anticipated, grabbing the attention of others in line. "I'm traveling alone."

The woman behind her backed away, closer to her husband.

Brianna's eyebrows lifted, creasing her forehead. Her feigned friendly tone quickly turned to aggravation. "Look lady, do you want the rental or not?"

Kate's head dropped in defeat. She swiped the keys in concession and signed the receipt.

She turned away and pushed through the holiday travelers, using her carry-on like a snowplow. Her overstuffed suitcases gyrated behind her and threatened to fall at any moment. It may have been ridiculous to pack the snow boots, but she'd rather be beaten with them than admit she would not use them.

She'd never give Eric the satisfaction.

"Excuse me," she mumbled, as she worked her way through the crowd to the exit.

She groaned as she passed all the Christmas lights and garlands hanging from the ceilings while traditional Christmas music played in the background. She practically ran toward the doors, but as soon as the sliding glass doors opened, she immediately stopped. The cold slapped her face like a frozen glove. Snow whipped her hair, thrashing it against her face.

She dug in her pockets for her gloves, but remembered stuffing them somewhere inside her suitcase with her boots, and she had already forgotten where she put the rental keys. With a grunt, she dragged her bags through the cold, wet, white, mess, patting down all twenty pockets in her new ski jacket as she reached the silver minivan. When she recovered the keys, her fingers could no longer bend as she fumbled at the fob to unlock the doors. She pulled the handle, but the driver's door wouldn't budge. The passenger's side door was also frozen shut. With her coat sleeve, Kate wiped the snow off the window. She could see an ice scraper on the back seat.

Of course.

As she stared inside the minivan with the snow churning around her, she had never hated her life more than in that moment.

With her credit card, she chipped away enough of the ice to get the passenger's sliding door open. Her designer leather boots now sported a salty white mark along the top stitching.

She fell into the van, thankful for the shelter. A text chimed from the belly of her purse. She dove for her phone, digging around in each pocket.

Great work, O'Neil! Clients extremely happy. I'm sending you on vacation more often!

A sinking sensation of regret weighed her down. Emotions pierced every nerve in her body as she looked at her boss's words. How was she going to keep pretending?

Christmas was two days away. If she told her mom or sister that Eric had left, it would be game over. They'd never be able to forgive him. Her mother's motto: Trust no man.

And what if Eric changed his mind? What if he just had cold feet, and came back?

"No more thinking," she said aloud. She had a week to figure things out before she had to go back home. Until then, everything would remain the same. Even if that meant pretending to be with Eric over the holidays in Camden Cove.

She threw her phone on the passenger seat and took another deep breath. With both hands she pulled back her damp, wildly out of control curls into a ponytail and took off toward the entrance ramp.

Brake lights lined the interstate as she pulled onto the highway. Creeping along, there was no movement in sight. Her cellphone sat dangerously close to her in the next seat. Would Eric call to check in with her? To make sure she made it? To see if she was okay after he'd broken her heart?

The traffic crawled around the edge of the city of Portland. She recognized some of the buildings from when she was a kid. The coastal city hadn't changed much in fifteen years. Long docks jutted out into the water. Anchored boats rocked back and forth in the harbor with the storm. As she drove over the Back Cove Bridge, the sky, the sea, and the snow all blended together into a single shade of gray.

The traffic moved slowly and with each tap of the gas, the minivan fishtailed in the snow. So much for all-wheel drive. With each inch forward, she squeezed her hands tighter around the wheel, focusing on the tire tracks in front of her. Visibility became worse as the afternoon sun snuck away. Even the snow and the traffic didn't stop her thoughts from spinning around and around in her head. Her life, as she knew it, had ended.

She had spent months looking forward to showing Eric where she spent all of her childhood summers and winter holidays. Camden Cove was magical to her. Snuggled up against the coast of Maine, the small village had miles of rocky beaches to explore and swim, quaint shops and restaurants, and her aunt Vivi's cape all nestled in along the cove. It was like living in a fairytale.

Now it would be her refuge from the reality that she and Eric were over. Forever.

Then another heart palpitation made her grip the wheel, and after two hours and four heart attacks later, the exit for Camden Cove finally appeared. She had hoped that once she reached the village, it would give her some relief, but it hadn't. The breaths she struggled to take just became harder as she exited off the interstate.

However, once on Main Street, the little town turned in a winter wonderland, glistening in lights and snowflakes. Even with the storm, people were out Christmas shopping. The classic New England grey-shingled buildings were all aglow. In the prime hour of the evening commute, the road was packed with vehicles and people. Christmas wreaths hung from the street lamps, business doors decorated with holiday flare, and a tall Christmas tree lit the village square. She squinted to see a lobster holding a star at the top.

As she passed the old hotels and inns, she strained her neck and leaned forward in her seat, trying to find the one thing she had looked forward to since leaving Minnesota... the ocean. But even with the familiar twists and turns along the edges of the Atlantic, she could not make out the water through the snowflakes falling from the sky.

When she passed the white Congregational church, she knew she had less than a mile to go. The last bend curved up a steep hill toward Prospect Street. As she pressed the gas, the wheels slipped to the shoulder. The van slid dangerously close to the ditch that dropped at least six feet down the hill. Somehow she managed to steer the van back onto the road, but just as relief swept in, a snowplow thundered out of the adjacent road before she had time to move to the right side. Its giant blade rumbled head-on toward her, and the noise was startling. In panic, she slammed her foot on the brake, but there was no stopping. She swerved the van to the left and nose-dived into the ditch. The metal groaned as it hit the frozen earth.

She would never drive a minivan again.

~

The phone rang, and Matt Williams put down his cup of coffee. With the snow coming down, he shouldn't have been surprised he'd be called out, but he was, nonetheless. A snowstorm wasn't going to keep any Mainer from their Christmas shopping.

"Turner Towing."

"Hey, Matt." It was Susan, the roadside operator. "A woman in a minivan is off the road on Prospect by the fire station. She needs a pull."

"Got it." Matt grabbed his coat off the back of his chair. "I'll head over."

He hung up and grabbed the keys to the truck. He couldn't remember why he agreed to do this side gig for his friend Dan. He'd rather be out on the Atlantic than having to drive a tow truck in the biggest snowstorm of the year. Even with all the warnings, someone always drove too fast or recklessly through the snow. One thing he learned early on in his fishing career was to never underestimate a storm, especially a nor'easter.

He jumped into the truck and let the engine warm up. No need to rush, the woman was just a few miles away. The truck moaned as he pulled into reverse, the tires crunching through the snow. In only a couple hours' time, almost a foot lay on the ground, and it didn't look like the snow was stopping anytime soon. It stuck to every surface. He could barely make out his headlights through the flakes.

Just like Susan said, a minivan flashed its hazards up past the fire station. It was a bad spot to get stuck, but he'd get her out of there in no time. She hadn't gone too far into the ditch.

Pulling his jacket's hood over his head, he jumped out to inspect the damage. The woman watched him through the side mirror. He gave a quick wave and went around to the passenger side to check the right wheel. It was lodged in the snow, but nothing the tow truck couldn't handle.

He walked up to the window as she rolled it down. "You alright?"

She nodded. A low glow from the dashboard lit her face. "Thank you so much for coming."

"You're welcome." Matt leaned further inside the car when he recognized her. Katie O'Neil was back in town after all these years. His mother mentioned she was coming for the holidays, staying at her aunt's place, but he never expected to see her. He certainly never expected to be pulling her out of a ditch.

"Katie O'Neil, you look exactly the same." He smiled at the coincidence, but her face appeared startled. "It's me, Matt."

He ran his hand through his hair as he pulled off his baseball cap.

"Matt?" Her eyes widened. "How are you?"

Matt settled further into the window. "My mom mentioned you were staying in town for the holidays." His mom never let him forget that he had a thing for Katie back in the day. He looked beyond her into the car. Where was the fiancé?

"Oh." She looked away, cutting off eye contact.

Adrenaline swirled inside him like the flakes falling down from the sky. After fifteen years, she still got to him. Long lost memories flashed through his head. Things he hadn't thought about in years.

Matt snapped back to reality. "I don't see any damage except a few scratches. Maybe a dent or two. You can sit in my truck while I pull your minivan out of the ditch."

Her hands slapped her face before he noticed her shoulders shaking. It took him a minute to realize what she was doing. Was she crying? Heavy sobs, to be exact. What the…?

Matt didn't speak, but stayed still. He had seen people become emotional in accidents, but this wasn't even an accident. She and the car were fine, but she cried like her whole world had fallen apart.

"I reserved an SUV!" she cried into her hands. A low moan came from deep inside her, and she sounded like a dying animal.

He'd never admit it, but he'd imagined what it might be like to see her again. Katie O'Neil was the one who got away. They may only have been teenagers, but he never stopped thinking of her. Though he'd never imagined their next encounter to be like this.

He noticed the large diamond ring on her finger. So he was right about the fiancé.

He wished with everything he knew what to do in a moment like this. His sister would be in the car, wrapping her arms around her, listening. His brother would have helped her somehow, but all he did was stand, unsure what to do.

He waited a few moments before asking, "Are you going to be okay?"

She sniffled and nodded her head as she hiccuped a breath.

"I'll get you out of here in no time, but you need to sit in my truck or stand by the side of the road while I pull you out. You can't stay in your…" Matt paused before saying, "vehicle."

She nodded and wiped her eyes with both hands. She pulled out a tissue from her purse and blew her nose before opening the door and getting out. They jogged to the tow truck and he opened the door for her.

"Thanks," she said as she climbed into the passenger's seat, but she didn't look at him.

"No problem." Matt put his hat back on. "Let me hook up and I'll pull you out. You'll be on your way in no time."

Her eyes watered up as she looked at the van. "Is there any way I could pay you to tow the car to my grandmother's?" Her voice cracked. "I don't want to drive anymore."

Matt had towed plenty of vehicles, but never so the driver didn't have to drive. He couldn't say no, not with her eyes brimming with tears.

"Sure thing, stay tight." He closed the door and got to work. As soon as the vehicle was secured to the truck, Matt hopped in the driver's side. He brushed off the snow from his cap and blew his breath into his frozen hands.

"Hope you have plans to stay in tonight. This storm looks like it will stick around for a while," he said, as he put the truck into drive.

She looked the other way out the window. "I have no plans."

He could've hit himself in the forehead when an awkward silence fell between them. Normally, he could make small talk with just about anyone, but she avoided eye contact, so he stayed quiet the rest of the drive. He wasn't sure if she'd start crying again. Maybe it was the culmination of everything, with traveling through the storm and sliding off the road that made her this upset. Or she had become extremely dramatic over the years.

When he reached Riverside Lane, he backed the truck into the driveway. "It'll just take a few minutes to release your vehicle."

Katie nodded, and before she opened the door, she said, "Thank you for bringing me home."

She jumped out of the truck and walked through the snow, leaving a trail. She opened the garage door, ducking underneath and out of sight. By the time the door was completely open, she had already gone into the house, leaving Matt behind in the snow.

"Good to see you, too," he mumbled.

It only took a few minutes for him to drop the minivan. He drew up the receipt on the portable printer and walked toward the front door. He glanced in the window and saw Katie standing under the kitchen light. Her head tilted back as she took a drink from a bottle of amber-tinged liquor.

She's still interesting.

He walked up to the front door. Smiling, he rang the bell, still reeling from pulling Katie O'Neil out of a ditch. When she opened the door, he waved. "Your vehicle's all set. I can take either cash or credit."

"Oh right, sorry." She looked around the foyer and grabbed her purse from the floor.

As she dug in her bag, he looked out to the snow so he wouldn't stare at her. He had so many questions he was dying to ask, but hesitated. He remembered hearing she worked as a graphic designer in Minneapolis. Her aunt told him about the engagement, but Vivi stayed in Florida for the winter. Why was Katie in Camden Cove, all alone on the holidays?

"Here you go," she said, handing him her card. The large diamond sparkled from her finger.

He grabbed the card from her, his fingers slightly brushing hers. He tried to ignore the heat running up his neck as he ran the card. He noticed his path through the snow to the front door had been almost covered up by the small ice pellets spitting down. He should get off the road himself, before too long. He handed her the machine to sign. The soft light lit up her face.

"Are you staying in town long?" he asked.

She bit her bottom lip and shook her head. A lone tear fell down her face. She said nothing more, just passed the machine back to him.

Feeling more awkward at her silence, he said, "Merry Christmas. It was good seeing you again."

She nodded only once and said as cold as the snow outside, "Merry Christmas."

She backed away into the house and shut the door.

He shook his head as he walked back to his truck. He turned and snuck one last peek back at the house, but no longer saw her.

"Welcome back, Katie."

As soon as she shut the door, she checked her phone.

Nothing.

Her body shook against the front door. Her chest heaved up and down hard as she tried to maintain control, and it hurt. She hurt everywhere. Every muscle was sore from holding in her worst fear.

He had really left her.

He hadn't called or texted. Even if she was having a temper tantrum, going on their vacation alone, didn't he want to know if she was okay? Didn't he care about her anymore? Or had he completely cut her out of his life?

She went straight into the kitchen and grabbed the bottle of whiskey her aunt kept above the oven. She didn't bother with a glass, just took a straight pull from the mouth of the bottle. She put the whiskey on the counter and slid down against the cabinets, sitting on the floor. The snow from her boots created a puddle of water on the tile and the cold wetness seeped into the seat of her pants, but she didn't move.

Christmas Eve was tomorrow, and she would be alone. She had never spent the holidays by herself. Holidays were meant to spend time with family. Eric was supposed to be her family.

She picked herself up off the floor and went straight to the sliding doors, pulling them open. The wind and cold gusted around her as she let the snow and sounds come in. One after another, like a clock ticking off time, the waves pounded into the granite cliffs below. She had imagined this moment for so many months since planning their vacation, but never once did she picture herself standing here alone.

That's when she saw the lights from the tree. In the corner of the room, in front of the bookshelves, a small potted pine tree sat, decorated, and with a shiny red present sitting underneath. She picked it up and read her aunt's handwriting. "To the happy couple."

She crumpled to her knees, dropped the gift to the floor, and let the tears fall.

CHAPTER 2

The sun glared off the freshly fallen snow and burned into Kate's eyes. She tried to keep sleeping, but the nagging sickness in her stomach made her wake up. Her hand clutched her phone, and she was still in last night's clothes. At some point, she must've passed out, because the Nina Simone album spun on the turntable of Gram's record player, and all the lights were still on. Her head was killing her.

She pressed the home button on her phone. Only the time and date were displayed on top of the picture of her and Eric hiking.

She couldn't believe he hadn't called or at least texted her. It had been almost two days. They had never gone that long without communicating.

Until now.

Would she never talk to him again? Never hear his voice? Never feel the warmth of his breath?

When she first left their apartment, she hoped she would receive a call from him by the time she arrived at the airport in Minneapolis. He would tell her he was sorry, and that he was on his way. When it was time to board and the call hadn't come, she hoped he'd run toward her at the gate. When she boarded the plane, she imagined he'd find another flight and text her with the details—maybe even show up at her aunt's door, begging for forgiveness. But as the night turned into a new day, Kate's hope vanished.

They were really over.

One last desperate thought ran through her head when she saw the snow piled halfway up the glass doors. Maybe the weather prevented him from traveling. He could be stuck in Minneapolis because of the storm. Maybe he couldn't get hold of her.

Her phone vibrated in her hand and she jolted up.

It was ringing.

The screen read *Mom's Cell*.

She turned her phone off and fell back onto the couch. She couldn't avoid her mother forever, but she couldn't afford to lose it again. God knew what Matt Williams thought of her after last night's hysterics. Apparently, her trigger to lose her sanity was the word 'minivan'.

She dropped the phone on the coffee table, wishing she had stayed in Minnesota. She had spent months convincing Eric to take time off and spend Christmas in Camden Cove. Had he been thinking about leaving her since then? Was that why he kept changing his mind?

Camden Cove might be a summer destination to most people, but Christmas was Kate's favorite season in the small village. Lights hung around the white-trimmed windows, wreaths graced every door, and window boxes overflowed with garlands. Santa even came to town on a lobster boat instead of his sleigh. Fireworks sparkled the night with lights on New Year's Eve. There was no better place to celebrate the holidays.

She begged Eric to go when Aunt Vivi offered them the house for the holidays. When he finally conceded, she planned everything—skiing up north, sightseeing in Boston, and New Year's at a five-star restaurant called The Fish Market. But mostly, her plans consisted of nestling around the fireplace, listening to the ocean together. Now, her dream vacation had turned into a nightmare.

True love was as real as Santa Claus.

She leaned into a sitting position, pushed up off the couch, but immediately sat back down. Her head felt heavy, and she needed something in her stomach or she was going to be sick. With all the hurt and travel, she had forgotten to eat.

She stood up slowly, allowing her head to catch up with her body, and took a deep breath. She shuffled her way toward the kitchen. Her aunt's warning flashed through her head as she opened the empty refrigerator. She had been in Florida for at least a month. There would be no milk or cream for her coffee. There was only dry cereal and oatmeal in the pantry. None of those options were going to work.

She needed grease. And bad.

Grabbing her ski jacket, she peeked out the front window. There had to be a few feet of snow out there and even from inside, she could tell the road hadn't been plowed yet. The mini-van, with her luggage still inside, could barely be seen under the coat of white. Her only option was to trek over the footbridge into the village. There had to be something open that could give her a cup of coffee and food to ease her stomach.

Kate rummaged through Vivi's hall closet and found a bright yellow hat with matching pom-pom, an equally bright scarf in a different shade of yellow, and a pair of moon boots she swore were bought in the early eighties. It would do for the short walk to the village.

Matt glided his boat, Maggie Mae, toward the harbor. Her bow didn't quiver in the choppy waters. The predicted nor'easter lived up to its reputation. On shore, white crystals shone off every surface in the sunlight. He adjusted his hat's visor, but it did little to shade the glare from the snow.

He rubbed his hands together to warm them, letting go of the wheel for a moment. The heater in the wheelhouse didn't help much on a day like today. He held a high respect for those who fished all year long on the Atlantic. If his mom didn't need the lobsters for the Christmas party, he wouldn't be hauling traps up in these icy waters after a storm.

Off in the distance, he could see another fisherman crazy enough to go out on the water. A boat he didn't recognize. Maybe someone who lost their traps in the storm. He squinted for a better look, but couldn't make out the name. Lobstermen rarely ran into a stranger. Everyone knew their neighbors, even on the water.

His phone vibrated in his coat pocket, distracting his thoughts. Most likely his mom, calling with instructions. Tonight was his parents' annual holiday party, when half of Camden Cove showed up to celebrate.

His mom went all-out for the event. Hence, the lobsters she requested for her signature mac 'n cheese. She had enlisted everyone's help, and had probably already begun cooking when he headed out at sunrise.

Take your time, she texted. **Dad says the roads aren't cleared**.

He rolled his eyes when he saw the kissing face emoji. A new trick she'd learned from his niece, Lucy. He'd head over once he pulled into the harbor.

He stuffed the phone back into his pocket, and an image of Katie O'Neil flashed through his head. Even a mess, she still looked amazing. Really amazing. Seeing her was like stepping back in time, making him feel like a teenager again.

Where was the guy from back home that Vivi had mentioned? It didn't matter, he supposed. Wherever Prince Charming was, he was one lucky man.

He looked out at the bow of the boat, steadily leading the way toward shore, the only woman that he could count on never leaving.

He imagined how Katie might see Camden Cove. He took in the picturesque scene of the village shoreline as though he was a visitor. He couldn't imagine living away from the water. Being landlocked would be suffocating. He needed to breathe in the ocean air and feel its dampness. Even as a small boy he knew he'd be on the ocean, instead of inside his parents' restaurant like his brother. He didn't think twice when the chance came to get his own boat. After he received his license, he spent everything he'd earned all those years, working twelve to fourteen-hour days busting his butt, and bought Maggie Mae. She was the most beautiful thing Matt owned, and completely worth depleting his finances, even if Justine, his ex-wife, didn't think so.

Off in the distance, something caught his eyes. A figure navigated over the footbridge, trudging through the snow. Enough had accumulated that the four-foot railings gave little support along the structure's sides. Who would be crazy enough to cross it? He strained to see through the sun's rays, and finally recognized her.

Katie.

What was she doing? Trying to get killed? He held his breath as she shimmied her way across the bridge, somehow managing to arrive safely on Harbor Lane. Her feet touched the street just as he saw the plow rumbling down the one-car lane. There wasn't much room for pedestrians even when a regular car drove through, but the plow didn't slow down to share the road.

She jumped up onto a store's front steps just as the truck plowed past her. Snow blasted her whole body as she stood frozen.

Then, she headed down toward the bakery. One of the only place opened in Camden Cove at this time of day.

Maybe he'd grab some breakfast before heading over to his parents' house.

~

"What the heck is with the plows in this town?" Kate mumbled to herself as she pounded her feet on the pavement, removing the residual snow that clung to her thighs. Her pathetic escape from the plow made her head pound harder and her feet more numb.

She glanced around the small village street. It looked just like when she was a little girl. Christmas decorations covered the weathered buildings, wreaths and garlands hung on the doors and windows, but instead of traditional ornaments, starfish and seashells rested among branches of pine. The street lamps were adorned with red ribbons and *Happy Holidays* signs. The town square's Christmas tree was wrapped with lights.

With all the beauty surrounding her, the magic of Christmas only made her feel sicker. As she passed each storefront, she saw *Closed* signs hung in the windows. She peeked in the windows of the tiny bakery named La Patisserie. There sat a five-tier wedding cake decorated with a bride and groom on top.

"You've got to be kidding me." First the minivan, now her perfect French wedding dessert course. The universe was telling her she would die alone.

With no other choice, she opened the door. A bell chimed against the glass and alerted a man behind the counter.

"Good morning," he said with a smile. "You braved the snow. I wasn't sure if we should even open."

She looked around the empty room.

"It's pretty rough out there." She patted the remaining snow off her jeans as she walked toward the wooden display cases. Pastries were lit by Christmas lights, with white chalked name tags nestled in front. Flaky croissants, pastel macaroons, blueberry scones all lay upon linen napkins. On top of the counter, caramelized buns with roasted walnuts sat on a silver platter. Baskets with loaves of bread and mini chocolate cakes sat on a glass stand. Melody Gardot's tenor voice sang carols to the notes of an accordion in the background. The tiny shop felt like a real Parisian patisserie. Everything looked divine, but it was not exactly the food she was looking for. At least she could get coffee.

18

"Do you offer anything other than what's on display?"

"Not usually, but what are you in the mood for?" the man asked.

She hesitated at first, but her stomach twisted and rose in her throat. "Do you have anything with grease to go with a very large cup of coffee?"

The corner of the man's mouth lifted, and he turned toward the back. "David, whip up a New Englander!"

"A New Englander?" The kitchen door swung open. A man wiped his hands on an apron that sported a lobster in a Santa hat. "Who doesn't want to try my Christmas Eve pain au chocolat?"

They both faced her and waited for her to respond.

She didn't know what to say except, "I'm Kate."

"You must be Vivi's niece! She said she'd send you our way." The man behind the counter offered a handshake. "I'm Frank, and this is David."

Her stomach lurched as she forced a smile. She wasn't sure how long she could make small talk. "Nice to meet you."

"You're just as beautiful as Vivi described," David said. He also extended his hand. "We just adore your aunt."

A smile came naturally at hearing that. Everyone fell in love with her eccentric aunt Vivi, with her spunky personality. "Yes, she's amazing."

Vivi had probably told the whole village she was coming to town. After breakfast, she'd stay inside the house until she flew back home—which would be as soon as she could. Staying here did nothing besides prove she was more pathetic than she ever thought.

"I'll whip up that New Englander for you," David said, walking back to the kitchen. "But try my pain au chocolat. You won't be sorry."

Frank smiled and handed her a mug. "Please help yourself."

With a little sugar, she filled her cup with dark roast. She grabbed the thick cream and lightened the dark liquid. Taking a sip before finding a seat, she settled at the furthest table from the counter.

She silenced her phone, setting it on the table, but it buzzed and lit up with messages, killing her softly each time. Work again. The office crisis in Minneapolis had followed her to Maine, even on Christmas Eve. Twenty-four hours ago, the Merrill design catastrophe had been the worst of her problems. She'd give anything to go back in time.

Frank set a chocolate croissant in front of her. "On the house."

"Oh, thank you, but I couldn't." She pushed the plate toward him, but he stopped it with his hand.

"Anything for Vivi's niece." He walked away without another word.

She frowned, thinking about how long it has been since she had talked to Vivi. Too long. Every summer until she was eighteen, she had spent from Memorial Day to Labor Day in Camden Cove.

Thinking back to all those summers, she bit into the pastry and before she knew it, she licked the remaining chocolate off her fingertips. The chocolate blended right in with the buttery dough and melted in her mouth.

Off in the distance, a boat's bell echoed in the cove, and the deep breath she had been struggling to take all morning finally came. The noose loosened around her rib cage, but tightened back up again. The more she fought, the more her lungs resisted. She focused on a red boat floating in the water.

One, two, three, but the noose only tightened.

She had become *that* woman.

The woman she so proudly declared she would never become.

The woman who crumbled when a man left her.

But never did she imagine her happily-ever-after to end the way it did.

"Told you."

Her stare broke away from the boat as Frank replaced her

empty plate with a new one. She tried to think of something to say, but words wouldn't come. Instead, she faked another grin.

"Two eggs over easy, a couple of bacon strips, home fries, toast, and a small stack of pancakes." He set the silverware next to a glass bottle of maple syrup. "Can I get you anything else?"

Her stomach's threat to heave alleviated as soon as the aroma of the comfort food hit her nose. "No, thank you. This is more than enough."

"Well, let us know if you do." He turned away as the bell hit the door, alerting him to a new customer.

She grabbed the maple syrup and dumped it over her pancakes before cutting her fork into the cake heaven.

"I didn't know you did made-to-order?" a man said, stomping on the wooden floors.

"Only for our special customers," Frank teased. "What can I get you, Matt?"

She stopped mid-bite. It couldn't be Matt Williams again, could it? She slowly turned.

Matt gave a little wave as his eyes met hers. His eyes were the same color as the sea glass she had saved in a jar back home. A green so deep you could swim in them.

"Mornin'."

She nodded, her mouth stuffed with pancake. His smile grew with her surprise. He was even taller than she remembered, over six feet, with broad shoulders. He wore a navy hooded sweatshirt with the words "Lobstah Man" printed on the back. She couldn't help but notice how his worn jeans fit him perfectly from behind. He was as handsome as he had been as a teenager, except now instead of peach fuzz, he had a full beard. His dirty-blond hair curled out from underneath his worn Red Sox cap. She prayed she didn't look like she felt.

He took a mug from Frank and filled it up. Then, to her horror, he sauntered over and took a seat at the next table. He leaned back in his chair, crossing his legs, and faced her. "So, you survived the storm?"

She swallowed. "Yes, thanks again for helping me out last night."

He sipped his coffee, but it did little to hide the smirk behind his cup. "No problem."

She stared at her plate, wondering if she should eat, or talk. What should she say to the guy who was her first kiss? And first heartbreak?

"How long are you in town?" he asked.

She shrugged. Honestly, she didn't know. New Year's Day, if she stuck to her plan, but hopefully only hours, if the airlines would accommodate her request to change flights.

Matt nodded. He leaned back in his chair and said nothing more.

"Will we get to meet that fiancé of yours while you're in town?" Frank asked, as he placed a plate in front of Matt.

"Um, I'm not sure." Was she kidding herself, holding out hope that Eric might still come? The thought of him not showing up made tears spring to her eyes.

"Oh," Frank said, looking puzzled. "Did he get stuck in the—"

"You and Uncle David need any help with the desserts tonight?" Matt interrupted.

Frank shook his head. "David's already made everything." Frank pointed toward the back. "What did you make for tonight?"

David's head popped out from behind the kitchen window. "I have a Buche de Noel and a pumpkin maple trifle. I'm making Grandma Grace's butterballs right now. Does your mom need something else?"

As their conversation continued, she returned to her breakfast, dunking her toast into the egg yolk. The bread was thick and doughy and perfect. Her stomach was already thanking her.

Matt said, "Hey, I was going to tell my mom to extend an invitation, but since you're here, why don't you join us tonight?"

It took a moment to realize Matt was talking to her.

"You should go," David called from the back. "The whole town will be there. My sister-in-law throws quite the party."

Kate swallowed and shook her head. "Oh, I don't think so."

"Come," Frank said. "It's a really nice evening."

"Bring your fiancé!" David yelled.

The breath she struggled so hard to keep steady slipped away. The tears stung her eyes and she used everything she had to hold them back, but it wasn't meant to be. One escaped before she could wipe it away.

"The weather really messed up everyone's plans." Matt put a clean napkin on her table. He stood up, bringing his empty plate to the counter. "I'll see you tonight," he said to Frank, then waved to David. He walked toward the door, but stopped before leaving and turned back to her. "We should catch up, sometime."

She mustered a smile, but couldn't look his way. Two breakdowns in less than twenty-four hours was a new record for her.

CHAPTER 3

*K*ate felt Frank stare at her from behind the counter. It wasn't a creepy stare, but more of a concerned one. The fact that she was the only customer made it difficult to eat without feeling self-conscious, especially since she teetered on having a breakdown in public again.

As she finished up, Frank walked toward her with a large white book in his hands.

"Vivi told us you're getting married." He placed the book on the table, flipping open the cover, revealing a photo album of desserts. "Have you planned your dessert course?"

She widened her eyes, hoping the tears would soak back in, but it was no use. She grabbed the napkin Matt had given her and dabbed her eyes.

"Was the New Englander that lousy?" he joked. "Are you okay?"

She nodded her head, but didn't respond, looking away.

"It's just that…" Her bottom lip trembled. "I don't need to plan a dessert course anymore."

Her heart plummeted at the truth. His face said he realized why she had come alone. Without knowing what was happening, he pulled out the chair across from her and sat down. At first she stiffened up, but then covered her face with the napkin, her shoulders shaking as she wept.

"I'm so, so sorry," she sobbed.

"There's no need to be sorry," Frank said, consoling her.

She lowered the napkin, looking at him as tears fell off her chin. "He said he couldn't do it. What does that mean?"

Frank shook his head. "What a horrible thing to go through, especially during the holidays."

"I didn't see it coming." She blew her nose. "He didn't even explain."

She wept again, heavy sobs with intermittent gasps of breath.

"He didn't even give you a reason?" Frank sounded upset for her.

"We were packing to come to Camden Cove when he just stopped and told me he couldn't do it." She spoke through hiccups. "I thought he meant flying out here, but then he said he… he couldn't marry me."

"You must've been devastated," Frank said.

She took a deep breath. "This was such a stupid mistake, coming out here. I wanted to prove that I was this strong, independent woman, but instead I've completely fallen apart. And now I'm falling apart in front of a complete stranger."

"Well, we're not strangers anymore." Frank tilted his head and took a long look. Her emotions were so raw, she was sure he could feel her pain radiating through her. "Never doubt your strength. You just being here, getting on that plane without him is strength."

He patted her hand, giving a small smile.

Her chin quivered. "I've lost my soulmate."

"He's not your soulmate," he said matter-of-factly, and leaned back in his chair. "Not if he's willing to leave you."

His words made her bottom lip tremble even more.

"Sorry. What I'm trying to say is that everything happens for a reason."

She felt sicker at hearing the terrible cliché.

"Sometimes when things fall apart, they're really falling into place."

He was not helping, even though her hiccups had slowed down. "I should go."

"Are you sure you're okay?" Frank asked as he stood up. "You should come to the party tonight."

She shook her head. "I clearly shouldn't be out in public."

"Get some rest today," Frank suggested. "But this evening, you're coming to the Christmas party."

Kate's eyes widened. "Oh, no, I can't be around people."

Frank tsked and then said, "I'm not letting you be alone on Christmas Eve."

Matt lifted the coolers filled with the live lobsters into the back of his truck and shut the lift gate once they were secured. He had a few minutes before he needed to go over to his parents' house, so he headed to Teddy's Toyshop to grab his last gift. A horse figurine his niece had requested. Nothing like waiting until the last minute.

"Matt!" a voice called from behind.

Matt turned to see Officer Martinez jogging toward him in the parking lot.

"Alex, it's good to see you." Matt greeted his brother's friend with a hearty handshake.

"Tell me that's for tonight?" Alex asked, pointing to the coolers.

"The storm isn't going to stop Sarah Williams."

"I do love your mom's mac 'n cheese." Alex had been a regular at the Williams house since Matt was a young boy. He played baseball with his older brother Jack, and was a lifetime Camden Cove resident like the rest of them. "I actually wanted to give you a warning. The Coast Guard called us and told us to listen around. They've seen some vandalism with traps recently. People's lines have been cut over near Perkins Island."

"Do you know who it is?" Matt asked, concerned. Matt hadn't heard any scuttlebutt about traps being messed with, but Perkins Island was part of his territory. He was sure he would know by tonight. Half of the town would know the details by his parents' party.

"You'll find out before us," Alex replied. Matt heard the undertone in his statement. Lobstermen had a long history of resolving matters between each other. "Would you let me know if you see or hear anything?"

Matt nodded. "Will do."

There hadn't been something like this for years, not since his grandfather died. For generations, territories were passed down within families. But some Fishermen believed one had to earn their place, and some thought Matt skipped to the head of the line without paying his dues, by inheriting part of his grandfather's territory.

Matt wondered whose lines were cut as he walked through the village's narrow streets, listening to the snow crunch under his feet. The morning was quiet, even the waves seemed softer. During the summer, this place was crammed with tourists. Cars lined the streets, traffic jammed the main strip, and every sidewalk or path was packed with folks visiting the quaint fishing town. He was proud to be a permanent resident, and even though most of his bread and butter came from those summer people, he preferred days like today when he had Camden Cove all to himself.

He opened the shop's door as a couple stepped out. He held the door, humming a Christmas carol, but stopped short when he realized who they were. Justine and Freddy were hand in hand, and appeared just as surprised to see him.

"Hey Matt," Freddy said, trying to be casual as he wrapped his arm around Justine. "Merry Christmas."

He ignored him, there was no need to carry on a conversation when one wasn't needed.

"I heard you're looking for some extra work this winter," Freddy said as Matt went to walk inside. "You know we always need help with maintenance and repairs for the hotel."

Matt gritted his teeth, but took the high road. "Thanks, but I'm good."

Justine didn't make eye contact. She stood holding a small bag, a present he assumed, in her hand. It wasn't until he took another look that he noticed the large diamond on her finger.

His face must've showed his surprise, because Freddy felt the need to tell the story. "I wanted to wait until Christmas morning, but I was so excited, I popped the question last night."

He locked eyes with Justine and said, "Congratulations."

She squeezed up closer to Freddy and smiled. "Thanks, we're thrilled."

He nodded, but added nothing else. What do you say to your ex-wife, who finally landed a man with the money she always dreamed of having?

"Tell your family Merry Christmas," Freddy said.

Matt squeezed the door handle, wishing he could squeeze Freddy's head instead. He swallowed his pride, got his niece's gift, and headed to his parents'.

Nothing made Sarah Williams happier than having her whole family at the house. Even though all her children lived close by, it was harder and harder these days to get them all together in one place at the same time. Christmastime was the exception.

His mom had an open-door policy for the Christmas party, but it was the usual crowd—mostly their family, some local business owners, and friends from the neighborhood and church. His brother would bring the prime rib, his uncles would bring the desserts, and he came with the lobsters.

When he walked in, Sarah called out to his dad, "John, Matt's here."

His dad looked up from his paper, then folded it, sticking it down beside the side cushion of his chair as he got up. "How many do you plan on prepping this year?"

"About a dozen... or two."

John gave her *the look*, and shook his head. "Two dozen?"

"It's not Christmas Eve without lobster mac 'n cheese." She sprinkled more salt into the boiling pot of water. "It's your family's tradition."

John wasn't buying it. She had grabbed hold of the tradition and made it bigger and more elaborate each year. She walked over to her husband, wrapped her arms around his waist, and kissed his cheek.

"I'll give a hand." John kissed her back, then put on his boots and headed out the door.

Matt and his dad carried in the coolers and dropped them next to the stove.

"Did you have any trouble getting this many?" she asked, surveying the load.

Matt shook his head. "Nah."

He sat on a stool along the kitchen's center island. Sarah didn't hold back with the holiday spirit. Wreaths hung on every window, with candles sitting on the sills. Hand carved snowmen and reindeer stood among pinecones on the side tables. Bowls of cranberries and jars filled with candy canes lined the kitchen table. She even convinced his dad to cut down a twelve-foot tree, the biggest one to date.

"So, guess who I ran into?" Matt said, grabbing a muffin from the basket on the counter.

"Who?" she asked, turning to the lobster. She dropped them one by one into the boiling water.

"Katie O'Neil."

"*The* Katie O'Neil?" She turned around to face Matt. She clearly remembered how head over heels he had been for her. "That's right. Vivi had mentioned she was coming into town with her fiancé."

"Well, she's here, but I don't think the fiancé came."

Her eyebrows lifted, and she wiped her hands with a dish-towel. "No fiancé?"

"No fiancé," he repeated. "I invited her to come tonight."

"That's nice of you."

"Who's coming?" John asked from his chair.

Matt swiveled to face him. "Vivi's niece is in town."

John opened the newspaper and nodded. "Is she bringing her whole family?"

Sarah stood, watching the pot. "Apparently she came alone."

"Just as long as I don't have to do any more for tonight."

"I wonder where her fiancé is." He could see Sarah's curiosity grow.

He shrugged. "She was at the bakery eating breakfast, so I'm sure we'll know the whole story soon, from Uncle Frank."

She thought about it for a moment as she grabbed a coffee mug and filled it, setting it in front of him.

"Got anything stronger?" he said, as he took a sip.

She gave him a look.

"What? It's Christmas Eve, after all." He walked to the fire-place and sat on the hearth. He leaned over and rubbed Maggie Mae, the family's chocolate lab.

"Everything okay?"

"Of course," he replied. "Just looking for something to warm me up, nothing else."

Just then, a car door slammed, and soon his sister Elizabeth walked into the kitchen. Her hands were full of Christmas bags and wrapped presents. Sarah rushed over to help her daughter as she stomped off the snow onto the floor mat. "Gentlemen, a little help?"

Matt and John sprang up.

"I have more in the car," Elizabeth said, setting the bags on the counter. "Did you hear?"

He knew before she said it, but shook his head.

"Freddy popped the question."

His stomach fell anyways, and he wished his coffee was stronger. "When did you hear?"

"She posted her ring last night." She grabbed a water bottle from the fridge. "I can't believe they'd get engaged this soon."

"Yeah, well, why wait?" He ignored the looks his sister and mother were giving him.

"What are you talking about?" his mother said.

"Justine and Freddy got engaged last night," Elizabeth said.

Sarah's eyes widened. "They're engaged?!"

The last thing he wanted to do was sit around and talk about his failed marriage, his cheating wife and her new engagement.

Just as Elizabeth's mouth opened, before she spoke, he interrupted and said, "Did you hear who's in town?"

CHAPTER 4

$\mathcal{T}$he afternoon light had begun to fade when Kate gave up trying to find a flight out of Maine. She talked to every person from the airline's customer service, but with the storm and the holidays, the earliest flight was in another two days.

She'd be alone for Christmas.

She sat in the middle of the floor with the contents of her suitcase spread out across the living room. She stared out the windows. Even as her life spun out of control, the view of the cold, gray water pulled her in. Everything seemed petty and insignificant as she watched the endless whitecaps spitting their fury in every direction as the wind blew.

With each chime and vibration her phone made, her heart leaped with hope that Eric was reaching out. She'd accept an apology. She'd even be okay spending the holidays alone, if everything went back to normal afterward.

All the messages were from work, however. Melinda, her office assistant, followed Kate's request to keep her updated on the progress of the Merrill deal, maybe a little too enthusiastically. Text after text of forwarded memos and emails came throughout the day. She even had the nerve to wish her a Merry Christmas.

She dropped her phone and wrapped her arms around her knees. Her throat ached as she tried to press her body into the floor. Hold it in, she thought to herself, hold it in.

Then the doorbell rang, and she popped up from the floor, hope filling her soul.

Eric.

She sprang from the floor and raced toward the door. Their romantic Christmas by the sea could still come true. Dinner by candlelight while they listened to the ocean.

She almost called out his name before she realized who was standing outside the front door. Frank peeked in the side window, waving as she came closer. David stood with his back facing the door, but she could tell he was holding dishes in his hands. They were true to their word. Frank had even donned a dinner jacket.

Oh no.

She had no business attending a Christmas party. They were lovely for insisting… and insisting… but even though her tears stopped flowing, sadness penetrated every ounce of her being. All she wanted to do was curl up into a ball, cocoon herself under blankets and forget about the world around her. She was not emotionally prepared to celebrate a holiday she wished would just pass by. Pretending with her mom was hard enough. She couldn't pull it off all night with a bunch of strangers. Each time she had been in public proved that.

As she opened the door, she began her speech to excuse herself from the party. "It's really nice of you for insisting, but I'm going to stay in—"

"Nonsense." David walked past her into the front hall. He held a tray in both hands. "We've attended this Christmas party forever. If we miss it this year, oh well. You're not spending the holiday alone."

Frank walked in after David and hugged her limp body. He held up a gift bag and handed it to her. "Merry Christmas!"

Kate stood helpless, holding the gift in her hands, not sure what was happening around her.

David walked straight into the kitchen and turned on the oven. "Do you know where Vivi keeps her blender?"

"Um…" She had no idea. "Maybe in the pantry?"

"We wanted to make sure you were alright," Frank said. His gaze went toward the suitcase. Clothes spilled out all around it. "Vivi would do the same."

"I don't think I'm up for—" The blender's high-pitched motor interrupted her. When the motor's scream dissipated, she said, "I'm really not in the mood."

David walked out of the kitchen with two martini glasses filled with a white liquid. Candy cane crumbles rimmed the glass. "I call it Winter Wonderland."

He handed her one of the glasses and gave the other to Frank. He then disappeared back into the kitchen.

She held onto the stem with both hands, hesitating. She didn't want to give the impression that she wanted them to stay, but the cool, thick, liquid looked like a milkshake. The light peppermint aroma wafted in the air and before she realized, she took a sip. "Oh, that's delicious."

"There's plenty more," David said, as he walked back into the room with a plate of chocolate-covered truffles. He held it out in front of her and said, "They go perfectly with heartbreak."

Kate smiled and accepted that they weren't leaving as she held the drink, with a piece of chocolate melting in her fingers.

"May I?" Frank gestured with his drink to one of the leather armchairs.

"Please," she said, removing her unused running clothes from the seat, throwing them back into the spilled suitcase on the floor. She set the drink and gift on the coffee table and grabbed all the loose items of clothing. "It's very nice of you both to check in on me…"

"Once David has an idea, nothing will stop him." Frank smiled, his look sympathetic.

She looked down at the pair of flannel pajama bottoms she had worn all day since she got back from breakfast. She wouldn't need the black chiffon and satin dress she'd splurged on at Nordstrom's. She usually didn't spend that kind of money on clothes, but it was the perfect dress for the dinner she had planned for the two of them on New Year's Eve. Dinner at a restaurant on the harbor. She had read about it in her foodie magazine and booked it months ago.

"Your aunt has one of the best views around." David faced the sliding doors that led to the back yard. The same windows Kate had stared out of for the past eight hours.

The sun had just about set, leaving a purple haze behind the black silhouettes of Camden Cove's businesses. Houses and trees intermingled with twinkling Christmas lights. The ocean's shoreline gently bowed, outlining the cove. The water had turned as black as night.

"Well," Frank said, "are you going to open it?"

She had forgotten about the gift. "Oh, right."

From inside the bag, she pulled out a hardcover book titled, *50 Boyfriends Worse Than Yours*. A smile escaped her as she saw the pleasure on Frank's face. David turned from the view with an equally delighted expression.

"This is very nice of you." She opened the cover and read the handwritten inscription: *New beginnings are often disguised as painful endings*.

A small moan left her lips. She didn't want it to be the end.

"Thanks," she said quietly.

She picked up her drink and took a long sip, giving herself a brain freeze.

"How you holding up?" Frank asked, innocently enough, but he had no idea how the question might trigger the bomb of emotions she tried so hard to hold in.

She exhaled a deep breath before saying, "I'm figuring that out."

David sat and pushed the plate of truffles closer to her. "You need to eat a good dinner and distract yourself from your thoughts."

She felt the familiar prickle in her eyes. He was right. Wasn't that the same advice that she'd had given her friends? Forget about him. Move on. She spun the stem of the glass between her fingers again. She could sit here, miserable, like she had all day. Or she could sit and eat homemade truffles. "Do you have more chocolate?"

An hour later, they had drunk their wintery drinks and eaten all the truffles. Even though she had every intention of making them leave, she enjoyed their company. David had a dry sense of humor, and Frank played along. And when the sudden jolt of reality hit her, reminding her that her life had fallen apart, their conversation provided the distraction she needed.

"How long has it been since you were last in Camden Cove?" Frank asked, as David returned to the kitchen.

"Not since I was in high school."

She couldn't believe it had already been more than fifteen years. The last summer before everything at home fell apart. She hadn't even thought of the irony. The moment she stepped off the plane that summer after meeting Matt, her life completely changed with the announcement of her parent's divorce and her father's new family.

Both of her parents had picked her up, and they took her out to dinner and broke the news. Her father had already moved out, and into her soon-to-be-step-mother's house. She remembered walking into their house and never feeling at home there again.

"What a beautiful dress." He nodded at her New Year's Eve purchase draped over the arm of the couch. "You should wear it tonight."

The idea of putting it on made her chin quiver. She shook her head and tried to smile. "It was for New Year's."

His smile dropped. "You know, sometimes we don't mean to hurt the people we love."

Kate wiped her nose with a tissue and shook her head. "He just didn't love me anymore. There's no other reason he could give."

"Men are jerks." David walked out of the kitchen, balancing three plates of food like a professional. Frank stood and grabbed the plate resting on David's forearm and the silverware squeezed between his arm and chest. "We think only about ourselves."

Frank nodded in agreement, pointed his silverware at the New Year's Eve dress and said, "Showing him you don't give a darn, looks good in a black dress."

As Matt sat in his parents' living room, he couldn't remember how many drinks he'd had, but he contemplated whether he should hold on to something to help him stand up. He wasn't sure how steady he was on his feet.

His cousin Jules rambled on about the lines being cut off his traps, blaming everything from jealousy over the successes of their family, to the new regulations coming from the state. "I lost fifty traps that had been soaking for only a day."

Matt shook his head at the thousands of dollars potentially lost.

"Now I have to pay for a diver if I want those traps back."

"The real question is, who's moving in?" his brother Jack asked.

People didn't know much about what happened to Jules' traps, but everyone assumed it was another lobsterman. Worse, it could be one of the many lobstermen that stood in his parents' living room that very night.

Lobstering was a world of contrasts. They lived and breathed the water, but it was the very thing that could threaten their life. He had sailed through storms that could make a grown man cry, and yet on its calmest day, it felt like the safest place on earth. The fishing culture had changed little in the past hundred years, yet nothing seemed to stay the same—the weather, the tides, the rules and restrictions. It was the connection between all of Camden Cove's residents, but the thing that could tear the community apart.

Fishing was the only thing he had ever wanted, and now the only thing he had.

"I saw Noah Callahan down at the docks the other day," Jules said. "He was asking who was staying out all season."

"Let's not jump to conclusions." Matt thought of the boat he saw earlier that morning. It didn't fit the timeline, but he wondered if it had something to do with it.

Just as Matt placed his hand on the armrest to guide himself up, he saw Katie. In a black dress of the kind you saw in magazines—not in Camden Cove. She looked amazing. Her auburn hair hung down, the ends of her soft curls tucked under against her bare back. His eyes traced down to her high heels that showcased her slender legs. His heart jumped in his throat as he, and the rest of the room, checked out the newcomer.

He smiled as soon as she made eye contact. She no longer appeared as upset as before, but he could tell she was uncomfortable. He watched as David and Frank walked the room with her. The two introduced her to everyone. Some even remembered her from when she had come during the summers. Elizabeth gave her a hug and introduced Adam. He had forgotten they had been friends as kids.

But she'd always be *his* Katie.

He could tell Katie grew more at ease the more Elizabeth talked. Leave it to his sister to make her feel right at home. With each new person his uncles introduced, her eyes would squint as she smiled at the new face. She'd laugh at the right times and seemed genuinely interested, as though she didn't have a care in the world. Enjoying the banter between neighbors.

He didn't understand women.

He tried to stop looking over at her, but he couldn't help himself. His eyes kept sneaking glances without him even knowing. Her shoulders were pulled back and she clasped a small purse in her hands. She appeared taller than she actually was. She kept pulling her hair over one shoulder. Even over the dull hum of conversation, he could hear her soft, adagio voice.

Screw it. He was going to talk to her.

As methodically as possible, Matt walked across the room to her. The only real obstacle was the dog lying in the middle of the floor. With each step, someone would turn around, and he'd get stuck in the typical pleasantries of small-town talk, like the amount of snow piling up, what his family was doing for the holidays, and what he thought about Katie O'Neil being back in town. Then the inevitable question, "How are you?" with pity in their eyes.

Katie, however, didn't have pity. She had a smile.

"Hey, you came," he said, once he finally reached Katie.

She took a deep breath and nodded. "Yes, it was very nice of you to invite me."

His sister's eyebrows lifted in her meddling way. His mom, along with his uncles, had their own looks. He felt sixteen again, with everyone making cutesy faces because he was talking to a girl.

"Let me help you put out the desserts," Sarah said to David, and disappeared into the kitchen.

Soon, another guest arrived and diverted Elizabeth's attention. She left him and Katie standing alone.

Up close, she looked even more beautiful. The faint smell of vanilla and something else he couldn't place, drifted in the air around her. He couldn't contain his smile. She still looked like the young girl he'd met at the beach all those years ago collecting sea glass, only more sophisticated.

"How've you been?" he asked.

She bit her bottom lip, and he regretted asking, but then the corner of her mouth perked up. "Kinda cruddy. You?"

He laughed. "Kinda cruddy. Want a drink?"

"Yes, please." She swept her hair around one shoulder and an urge to sniff the back of her neck came over him.

Luckily, before he did anything stupid, he turned and walked away. He shook his head all the way to the kitchen. It took a minute to collect himself as he grabbed two local IPAs, then returned to Katie.

"Merry Christmas." He twisted off the caps and handed her one, then lifted his beer to hers.

She clinked her bottle against his. "Merry Christmas."

After a sip, he rolled back on his heels. "So, my uncles got you here."

He wasn't surprised. He knew how persuasive they could be.

"They certainly don't take no for an answer... but they're very sweet for bringing me." She glanced in the direction of the dining room and whispered, "I'll probably excuse myself when they're not looking."

"I won't say a word."

He held up his hand in a *scout's honor* salute, and an awkward silence lingered between the two of them. He rattled things off in his head, not sure what to say.

Then she asked, "Did you ever get a lobster boat?"

The question took him by surprise. She remembered. "Yeah, I bought one about five years ago."

Her thumb picked at the label on her bottle. "I saw your sweatshirt this morning, and remembered how you used to always want to be a lobster fisherman."

"How do you even remember?" Matt tried to think what else she might remember.

She shrugged. "How do you forget something like that?"

He wanted to tell her how hard she was to forget, but held back. He'd be a fool not to notice the diamond ring on her finger. The fiancé must've gotten stuck in the snow. A big meltdown for a missed flight, but it was Christmas, he guessed, and to end up alone would be disappointing.

"So, I heard you're a graphic designer." He thought of other things he remembered his mom telling him.

"Sort of." She sipped her beer, not adding any more detail.

He tried to think up neutral topics to discuss as the silence grew. She clearly didn't want to talk, but before he could stop himself, he asked. "Any plans while you're here?"

He waited as she stared back, hoping he hadn't hit a nerve.

"No, not really." She shrugged. "I was thinking about going snowboarding."

"You snowboard?"

"No."

Interesting. "Do you have a snowboard?"

She shook her head. "Nope."

"You'll want to rent a helmet," Matt warned her. "If I remember correctly, your balance wasn't the greatest."

"I didn't say I was going on a surfboard." She laughed, but then placed her hand on his forearm, sending a wave of electricity through his body. "I'm sorry for my meltdown. I'm still really embarrassed."

If it was just the two of them, he'd tell her his own stories of shame, but with Frank and Sarah watching over them, he shook his head.

"There's no need to be sorry."

Then he saw the smile he'd seen all those years ago, the one that made his knees buckle. Maybe it was the alcohol mixed with the nostalgia, but it was hard for him to think straight with her standing so close.

They continued with the small talk. She told him where she ended up attending college. He told her about fishing as his grandfather's sternman for ten years before getting his license. He told her fishing stories. He made her laugh, which was much better than making her cry.

"Do you mind telling me where the bathroom is?" she asked.

"It's down the hall, first door on the right." He pointed to the hallway.

"Thanks for the beer." She gave a wave. "Thanks again for inviting me."

"You're leaving already?" He looked at the clock. Not even eight-thirty.

She shrugged, hesitating before saying, "I really am tired from all the travel and stuff..."

She trailed off, then headed in the direction of the bathroom. He watched as she walked through the room, and wondered where her fiancé was.

Frank walked up next to him and whispered into his ear, "He left her."

"What?" Matt spun around to face him.

"The fiancé." He crossed his arms. "He left her right before they were supposed to fly out."

He snuck another peek as she left the room. He felt terrible for her. No wonder she was so upset in the van last night. "That's awful."

Frank nodded, but he raised his eyebrow. "You two seemed like you were catching up."

"Yes." He could tell his uncle was up to something, as per usual.

"Perhaps there will be a rekindling between the two of you."

"The last thing I need right now is another complicated relationship."

Kate stood in front of the bathroom mirror and looked into her eyes. They were slightly bloodshot from all the crying, but her makeup was intact.

Never in her life did she think she'd be back in Matt Williams' home. Her emotions were at extremes. One minute a wave of grief washed over her, and the next she felt the warm familiarity of Camden Cove. Her mind spun like a whirlpool. A surreal deja vu mixed with the pain of reality.

Matt seemed exactly the same as the carefree surfer she'd met all those years ago, happy-go-lucky, living his days for the water. How she wished she could return to those summer days. Feel the naïve happiness of falling in love.

She splashed cool water on her face. A breath escaped. At least she still had her family, her friends, and a stable job. Was that enough, without him?

She held onto the edge of the sink and leaned closer to the mirror. She wanted to blame Eric for leaving her, but as she looked at her reflection, she realized she didn't know who to blame.

She snapped out of her thoughts when someone knocked on the door.

"Just a second!" As she headed back to the party, she noticed the house had a golden glow from all the Christmas lights. A nautical theme blended in with the holiday decor. She slowed by a table with framed photographs of the Williams family. Everyone carried the same photogenic gene, even the dang dog.

Matt walked over with a half grin. "How are you getting home? I could find you a ride."

"I'll walk back." She remembered the way. "It's only a couple of blocks."

He looked down at her feet. "But you're in heels."

She glanced down at her black shoes, regretting ever drinking that wintery dream David gave her. "I'm from Minnesota."

"Then you should know better."

His remark caught her off-guard, and a laugh escaped her. "Touché."

She spotted Frank and David. They stood behind the kitchen counter with Sarah, absorbed in conversation. A perfect time to sneak out.

She noticed Matt smiling at her. "What?"

He stuffed his free hand in his pocket and took another sip of beer. "I can't believe you're standing in my parents' home after all these years."

She wondered if he knew the story. How her fiancé had left her. He didn't let on. "Wasn't this the part of the barn?"

He pointed above them. "Yup. They moved the kitchen out here and redid everything, but kept the loft."

Her cheeks flushed as she looked up to a balcony. They had their first kiss up there, among old wooden lobster traps and fishing gear. They had dangled their feet over the wooden edge and looked out at the whole harbor.

"They've done a beautiful job." She checked on David and Frank, who were still distracted. If she wanted to get out of there, she needed to do it now. She'd thank them later. Turning to Matt, she said, "I think I'm going to sneak out now. Thanks for inviting me. It was really nice."

"Let me grab your coat for you, and I'll walk you home."

"No, I'll be fine."

"I'm sure you will, Minnesota, but I'd like some fresh air."

"You're as bad as David and Frank."

He led her down the hall to a smaller room in the front of the house. On the sofa, she found her coat and bundled it around her, pulling up the hood. As soon as he opened the door, the cold air rushed inside. They quickly stepped out so as not to let the warm air escape.

"The snowbanks are up to my waist already." She couldn't believe how much snow the town already had.

Matt followed behind her on the front walkway. "It's been a crazy start to winter."

The noise from the party dulled once they reached the road. Off in the distance, the waves sprayed the rock cliffs and the sporadic clanging of a bell clanged. Through the bare trees and houses, she could see the small town twinkling below.

Their footsteps crunched the packed snow underfoot as they walked. A few minutes passed before Matt broke the silence. "The water glows on nights like tonight."

"Hmmm." Her gaze fell on the water. It was true. The light from the waxing moon illuminated the clouds lingering from the storm. The whitecaps appeared fluorescent from their vantage point.

"Do you remember when I took you surfing?" Matt asked.

The image of her head smashing on the edge of the board flashed in her mind. "I'll never forget it. That's the first time I got stitches."

Matt laughed.

Her fingertips traced the scar on her forehead. "I believe you're the one who almost fainted."

He made a face. "There was so much blood!"

The image of Matt sitting on the beach as she used his towel for her head flashed through her mind. Once he recovered, though, he was her knight in shining armor. He took her to the emergency room, held her hand while the doctor stitched her up, and gave her a bouquet of wildflowers the next day. It was one of the most romantic gestures she had ever received.

As they approached her aunt's street the sidewalk hadn't been cleared, and Kate did her best to step over the embankment, but her heel slipped on a patch of ice and her leg swung out in front of her. Just as she slipped, Matt grabbed her elbow and swept his arm around her waist, steadying her on her feet.

"Thank you," she said.

He took a second to look into her eyes before he said, "You're welcome."

He slowed down as she walked up the steps to the front door, staying on the sidewalk.

"It was nice seeing you."

"You, too." He stuffed his hands into his coat pockets. "Merry Christmas."

"Merry Christmas." She gave a little wave and unlocked the door. Before stepping inside, she glanced back at Matt. He waved and watched her until she stepped inside.

Immediately, she rushed to the kitchen and reached for her phone, charging on the counter. She hesitated before she picked it up. Even as hard as it had been to pretend at the party, she was thankful that she had gone. Frank and David were right. There were a few brief moments where she wasn't obsessing about everything falling apart around her.

She stared at her phone's black screen, afraid to wake it up and be confronted by the truth. Had anything changed, or would the pain wash over her again? Her thumb pressed the home button and she scanned the names listed on the screen—texts from her family and friends. She didn't bother to read any of them. None of them were from Eric.

Without second guessing herself, she typed a message. **Merry Christmas**. It would be enough for him to know that she was reaching out. It was up to him from this point.

She pulled open the sliding door and started counting the waves, but Eric continued to sneak into her thoughts. What was he doing? Where was he? Who was he with before midnight on Christmas Eve?

Kate took off her dress and put on her pajamas, then started a fire. When it was crackling, she opened the windows. The tangy scent of salt permeated the room. She listened as the ocean waves crashed against the rocky shore.

She sat, twisting her ring around her finger, and studied it one last time. She eased it over her knuckle and pulled it off, placing it on the floor in front of her. Eric always had a great sense of style. Designer clothes, classic cars and diamond rings. It was beautiful. A round-cut stone set in a vintage French halo. She often stared at its beauty, not believing it was hers.

She first met Eric at the diner in downtown Minneapolis. She was sitting alone in a booth reading a book on her lunch break, when he slid across from her and introduced himself. He rambled on for over a minute, telling all about how he had attended business school in the east, started working at a bank in Minneapolis, but hoped to return to the suburbs of Chicago. She didn't say a word until he stopped to take a breath, and said to him, "I'm not Becky."

Kate laughed as his face dropped, clearly embarrassed. But even though his face reddened, he exuded confidence.

She immediately fell for him.

Since Eric had the same ambition in business as she had in design, she wasn't in a rush to get married. As she worked her way up as a graphic designer, he worked his way up in the bank.

And make her way she did. The small start-up she worked at suddenly had over a dozen employees, with Kate being officially vice president of design. It was everything she had worked for, but she secretly hated it. She no longer designed, she managed other designers. She loved her boss, Rodney, and the people she worked with, but she didn't like being middle management. The only reason she stayed was because with the new house and the wedding, she couldn't afford to think about switching to a new job, earning less. She thought getting married and having a home with Eric was all she needed.

There was only one time other than with Eric, that she'd been in love. Before her parent's divorce, when she believed life was full of possibilities and happily-ever-afters. The summer with Matt.

She had always known about Matt, the local boy from town. She and her sister Jen would walk from Vivi's house and cross the footbridge to the village. They'd buy an ice cream, or stop at the candy store. Matt was always on the periphery, hanging around Camden Cove.

But it wasn't until the summer, when she turned thirteen that she fell for the cute local boy. As she sifted through the sand to collect sea glass, he walked up to her, pushing his bike. He peeked inside her plastic bag and saw her meager findings.

"You need to go to Perkins Beach." He pointed toward the coastal trail.

She stood, covering her eyes as she looked down the trail. Her hair blew in her face. She had never gone that far away from her aunt's house.

"I could show you," he said, throwing his leg over the bike. He pointed to his handlebars. "You want a ride?"

She didn't move at first, not sure if she should go with him or not, but she wanted the colorful gems. The thrill of this cute boy offering her a ride to a beach overcame any doubts she had about not telling her aunt where she was going. She'd face the consequences later. She lifted herself up on the handlebars.

He rode her all the way down to the end of the trail and into a different neighborhood. Houses stood against the shoreline, nestled within tall bushes. The scent of beach roses perfumed the air. He pointed to a tall wooden structure with sticks hanging off its sides. "That's an osprey nest." Above them, a large bird circled the nest with a fish dangling out of its mouth.

He continued to pedal down the narrow streets lined with weathered cottages. Flowers in window boxes blew in the wind as they rode by, bouncing over every pebble and patch of sand. At the end of the road, he slowed down and she jumped off.

"That's Perkins Beach." He pointed to an inlet full of sand and shells. They were the only ones there, except a pair of seagulls picking at the ground.

She turned to him in surprise. "How come nobody's here?"

He dropped his bike in the tall sea grass, toasted from the sun, and started toward the water. "No one knows about this place, because the locals don't tell the tourists about it."

She loved the idea that he thought her worthy to share the village's secret beach. It looked as though it hadn't been touched for years. Large branches of driftwood were anchored on the shore. Shells and rocks had been washed up by the waves. Blackened seaweed, burnt from the summer's rays, covered the sand.

She followed him over a small footpath. As soon as she stepped onto the sand, she saw her first piece of glass. It was a frosted blue and the shape of a triangle. It fit inside the palm of her hand. Its rippled edge was dull from the ocean's tumbling.

"Look for light reflecting off the glass." He bent down, turned his head to the side and pointed ahead of them at a round, clear, circle poking out of the sand. They both ran toward it and dug it out. The round glass bottle was rough. "My whole life, I've never found a bottle washed up before. You must be lucky."

She held the glass treasure in her hands and studied the pores in the glass. "Not until I met you."

They spent the remainder of the day hunting. When they climbed up the rocks and down into their crevices, he'd hold out his hand to help guide her. By the time she needed to head back, they had found a full bag's worth. She didn't want the treasure hunt to end.

When he dropped her off at the public beach, she watched him ride away. That was the first time she had fallen for someone, and for three summers afterwards, she kept a look out for the Maine boy. Hoping he'd be where she and her friends were, praying he'd show up, and disappointed when it didn't happen. It wasn't until the summer when she turned sixteen that he once more showed up in her life.

Her sister had graduated high school and got a job to save up for college. Her mother found full-time work. The day she dropped Kate off at the airport, she wore a dress suit she had bought at Talbots and plain black high heels. She kissed Kate on the cheek and told her to help wash the dishes. She had a whole summer with just her aunt. The beach. And Matt.

It was the best summer of her life.

And then the worst.

Once she returned home, everything had changed. Her dad had moved out, her sister left for college, and her mother fell apart.

As an adult, she had been so careful with her emotions. Her mother complained that her father was a dreamer. She warned Kate to fall in love with someone stable. Eric was the very definition, and she couldn't even hold onto him.

She picked up her engagement ring and rolled the band between her finger and thumb. She couldn't keep wearing it. He hadn't reached out. She couldn't pretend with her family anymore that everything was alright, because everything wasn't alright.

The bells from the congregational church rang out, signaling midnight. Christmas morning had arrived.

She dialed her sister. Back home it was eleven, but Jen would still be up getting ready for Christmas morning.

"Hey, what's up?" her sister mumbled into the receiver.

"He left me, Jen. Eric left me."

CHAPTER 5

Kate woke to the sound of the doorbell. Vivi's bedside clock read five minutes past eight. She pressed the home button on her phone to make sure it was correct. Who was here?

Eric.

She flung the covers off, ignored the pounding in her head and rushed to the front door. He got a flight. She would have her Christmas after all. He still loved her.

She swung open the door and Matt stood there, wearing a Santa hat and holding a snowboard. "Merry Christmas."

She rubbed her eyes, not believing what she saw. He wore snow pants, boots and gloves. The cold swept into the house, and even in her flannel pajamas, she shivered from behind the door. What was he doing here?

As if he read her thoughts, he said, "It'll be crowded today, so we should get up there when it opens." He checked his watch. "It takes about an hour."

"What?"

"I'm taking you snowboarding."

"Did we make plans?" She may have forgotten a few minor

details from the party, but she'd remember making plans to go snowboarding.

"You mentioned you wanted to go, so I'm taking you."

"But it's Christmas."

"And it's one of the busiest days of the year. We should leave soon if we want a parking spot."

"Seriously? Whose snowboard is that?"

He looked at the snowboard, then back to her. "It's my sister's."

"What?" Kate couldn't believe what was happening. "I can't take your sister's snowboard."

"Sure you can." Matt held up a white bag with a red bow. "My uncle made some pastries."

"Don't you have plans with your family?" She tried to wrap her head around what was happening. Was Matt really standing on her doorstep on Christmas morning?

He shrugged. "I've been meaning to go, but never had a good excuse. Come on. I have a helmet and everything."

What was with that family and their powers of persuasion? Once again, she felt helpless. She stood there, speechless, and glanced down at her phone. No new messages had appeared since she checked the last time. Even after reaching out to Eric last night, he hadn't replied. He hadn't changed his mind. They were really over.

"I don't think—"

"David made almond and cheese brioches." Matt shook the bag.

A warm, nutty aroma drifted through the paper bag, triggering her appetite. Her stomach growled. Everything in her body told her to snag those brioches and crawl back in bed, hide under the covers and escape from the world. Snowboarding was the last thing she wanted to do, but as he held his sister's board with that smile of his, it suddenly seemed a lot better than crying all day.

"How long do I have to get ready?"

The right corner of Matt's mouth perked up. "If we leave soon, we can get there when it opens. I have a large coffee and a breakfast sandwich waiting for you in the truck."

"David made sandwiches, too?"

He shook his head. "No, I did."

He handed over the white bag. "You can eat these while you're getting ready."

She thought of the ski stuff still inside her suitcase. "I'll be as quick as I can."

He picked up the snowboard and tucked it under his arm. "I'll wait in the truck."

She leaned against the door, not believing what was happening. She rummaged through her suitcase, throwing clothes along the couch, stripping out of her pajamas as quickly as possible. She was going snowboarding, in Maine, on Christmas Day… with Matt Williams.

The first boy to ever break her heart. Or was it she who broke her own heart? She wasn't quite sure at this point. If she had hurt him, he was clearly over it. If anything, he felt sorry for her. His uncles had surely told her story by now.

As she pulled her wool sweater out, she noticed her journal stuffed at the bottom of her suitcase. Inside those pages was the detailed itinerary she created for the trip. She had made a plan for each day. She ripped the first few pages out, crumpled them into a ball, and threw them into the fireplace. Then, on a clean page, she began a new list. She wrote *snowboard* on top.

Check.

After three layers and a brush of the teeth, she slammed the front door behind her and jogged out to the truck. He passed her a warm package when she got inside, and backed out of the driveway as she bit into the sandwich.

"Are there hash browns in this?" she mumbled to him with her mouth full.

"My uncles aren't the only geniuses with breakfast foods."

She moaned with her second bite. It was exactly what she wanted. He passed over a large steaming travel mug.

"We'll be there in about an hour." He shifted the gearshift into drive, still wearing the Santa hat.

She couldn't believe she was doing this. She felt like a teenager again.

He pulled out a CD and inserted it into the stereo. It took a second to recognize the song. She could see him peeking at her as the music played, holding back a smile. "Is this my mixed CD?"

He nodded and sipped his coffee. "I have to say, I had forgotten how bad your music preferences were."

She laughed, cringing at the playlist. "I can't believe you still have it." She picked up the case sitting in the console. She recognized her teenage writing on the back, signed with a pink heart and her old nickname, Katie. "You're the only person who still calls me that."

"I like Katie for you." He drove the truck down into the center of town and stopped at the only light. "My sister found it in my old room, and hung on to it to give me a hard time." He tapped the wheel with his thumb. "After she saw you last night, she pulled it out. I still get teased about you, after all this time."

She hid her smile by looking out the window. "My aunt does the same. She always brings you up." She noticed his bare ring finger and said, "I thought you'd be married by now."

"I was." He drummed his thumbs on the steering wheel as the music played. "I got divorced."

And there's that good ol' foot in the mouth, she thought to herself. She regretted saying anything. She assumed that since he hadn't mentioned a wife, he wasn't married. She didn't think it would be because he had got divorced. "I'm sorry. I didn't mean to—"

"It's not tragic, just wasn't meant to be."

She snuck a glance. His eyes were on the road. She couldn't tell if she'd hit a nerve or not. He didn't add any more, and it wasn't any of her business. She wouldn't get personal again.

"Will I get killed out there today?"

It was a valid question.

His smile returned, and she instantly felt better. "Probably."

For the rest of the ride, their conversation remained neutral. He asked about her work, she told him about living in the Twin Cities. She avoided mentioning anything about Eric, and he didn't ask. Mostly they talked about fishing. The idea of living off the water, fighting the elements to catch lobsters, fascinated her.

"Do you wear the skipper outfit?"

Matt's face twisted in disgust. "First of all, no respectable fisherman calls it an outfit, and second, they're called Grundens. So yeah... I wear the skipper outfit."

She laughed. "I always pictured the guy on the frozen fish sticks box when thinking about lobstermen."

"You imagined that I looked like Gorton's Fisherman? He's wicked old." He shook his head. "Aren't you all fishermen in Minnesota, it being the land of ten thousand lakes?"

She liked his sarcastic tone. "It's more like 13,000, but no, I've never fished."

"You've never fished? Ever?"

"I grew up with a sister, and my dad never took me."

"Have you been on a boat?"

"Nope."

"All those summers in Camden Cove, and you've never been on a boat?"

"Nope."

"That'll have to change."

She couldn't hold back her smile. The thought of being at the helm of a ship sailing into the ocean's waves with the whole world before her, seemed to be exactly what she needed. Out in the middle of the ocean, away from everything.

When he pulled into the parking lot, attendants directed each vehicle around the snow-covered ground. She leaned forward and looked up to the top of the mountain. "How high is the beginner's area?"

"It's not too bad." He parked and then glanced up at the slopes.

He pointed to a hill in front of them. Groups of children gathered at the base. It made Afton Alps' black diamonds look like bunny hills.

He opened his door and jumped out. He walked to the back to grab the equipment as she pushed herself out of the truck. The snow blinded her, and she lifted her hand to block the sun. Each slope was narrow and vertical. Some peaks couldn't be seen.

She was going to die.

He tossed her a helmet and pulled out the two snowboards. "You ready?"

"Nope." She gulped as she fastened her chin strap.

He slammed the lift gate, picked up the boards and headed towards the lodge. "There's no chickening out, Minnesota."

Kate stood on the snowboard as Matt held her up. She clung to his gloved hands as she shimmied her body to the edge of the hill. His own board sat on the racks at the bottom. After her first attempt at getting off the carpet lift failed, he stayed on foot.

"Please don't let go until I'm ready." She looked out beyond him down the hill. People were scattered around the beginner's area like ants at a picnic. Poor innocent targets, if she couldn't stop.

"You're going to be fine." He stepped back to give her more room to steer. "You just have to go for it."

She blew out a heavy breath and released her grip. She crouched, bending her knees as she pushed away. "Okay, here goes nothing."

At first, Matt ran beside her, but soon, she gained unwanted momentum and he faded away as small children came danger-ously close to her. Before she knew it, the snowboard sped down the hill like Clark Griswold's greased steel sled.

"Use your edges!" he shouted out after her, running to catch up.

She whipped her snowboard around, her hips perpendicular to the slope, but the motion cut the front edge of the board, and she plunged to the ground. Her body bounced twice against the packed snow before coming to a sliding stop. Ice scraped against her face.

She didn't move at first. The wind had been knocked out of her, and she struggled before she could take a breath. Slowly, she moved each body part to make sure there was nothing broken. She pushed herself up onto her knees as Matt ran toward her, a look of horror streaked across his face. That's when she noticed the blood in the snow.

He fell on his knees next to her. "Oh, shoot."

"What?" She felt a sudden pounding between her eyes. She pulled off her glove and immediately examined her nose by pinching the bridge between her fingers. "Ouch! Do you think it's broken?"

His face scrunched up as he pulled out a cloth he kept for wiping his goggles and handed it to her. She bunched it underneath her nose.

"You hit the ground pretty hard. We should bring you to the first aid office."

She kept the cloth under her nose as he helped take off her bindings and lifted her up on her feet.

"Anything else hurt?" The poor guy's face twisted and creased as he looked at her. It said it all. He was worried she'd have another meltdown.

There she was, dumped figuratively and literally, and it all happened in front of him... again. Suddenly, a laugh escaped and made her snort. Which hurt, but it made her laugh more, and Matt appeared even more frightened. She couldn't stop laughing.

"Are you going to be alright?"

"Do you think it's too early for a drink?"

A small grin appeared. "You definitely earned it."

Matt grabbed her board and stood. He held out his hand and pulled her up. She checked the cloth to see if the bleeding continued, but it looked like it had already stopped. As they walked down the mountain to the first aid station, he held his arm out, and she gladly took hold.

After her examination, even though it had swelled up to twice its normal size, the kind woman determined she didn't have any broken bones, just a big bump on the head. The swelling didn't stop at her nose, but continued around her eyes, and with three different shades of pink.

Matt put his arm around her shoulder once they left and steered her toward the lodge. "I think this calls for a Bloody Mary."

~

A couple of burgers and a Bloody Mary later, Katie's face had swelled up even more, as Matt predicted.

"My face and butt hurt."

"At least you know how to stop," Matt teased. "Once you get your edges down, you'll be sailing down the mountain."

"I think I'd rather watch from the lodge." She spun her glass in both hands. "I'm glad I tried, though. It was fun."

It pleased him that she hadn't checked her phone throughout the whole lunch. On the drive up, she had peeked at it continuously. Was she enjoying his company?

"If you have no other plans tonight, my mom makes an incredible Christmas dinner with all the fixings." He didn't want the day with her to end.

"Didn't your mom just throw a huge party last night?" she asked.

Matt leaned back in his chair. "Believe me, she'd have it no other way."

She contemplated for a while, giving him hope, but then shook her head. "Thanks, but I'd like to stay in, tonight." Katie glanced out the windows that faced the slopes. "I'm exhausted."

He decided not to push, wondering what the fiancé was

thinking. How could he leave her alone on Christmas? He excused himself to the bathroom, but snuck his credit card to the bartender to cover the bill. On his return, he saw that Katie had left a tip.

"You didn't have to pay," she said.

"It was the least I could do. After all, I'm the one who forced you to go snowboarding."

"You didn't force me. I accepted your invitation."

He stared into her hazel eyes for a second too long before she looked away. She played with her coaster, and he worried that he had made her uncomfortable.

It was hard not to look at her. Even with a swollen nose, she reminded him of the good old days, when he didn't have a worry in the world other than getting on the water. He wished he could go back and change things, fight harder for the things he loved.

"You ready?" she asked, getting out of her seat, breaking the spell.

He followed her out of the lodge to where she'd stopped, looking up. Thick, heavy snowflakes cascaded from the sky and landed softly on her eyelashes. The snow twirled around her as she stood there. A strong urge to pull her into his arms came over him. The feeling was fleeting, but caught him off guard. Was it the damsel in distress, or the reminiscing that was getting to him?

He continued to remind himself how clearly unavailable she was on the drive back, but the closer he got to Camden Cove, the more he dreaded dropping her off and going their separate ways. What was it about her that was making him react this way?

Lavender.

She smelled of vanilla and lavender.

"How long are you staying around?" he asked, as he pulled into her aunt's driveway, stalling.

"I don't know." She sighed. "I have no plans."

"Then come tonight." He tried again, but he could tell by the way she scrunched her face that she wasn't interested. He resorted to begging. "Come. Before another decade and a half, passes."

Katie bit her bottom lip. "How about a boat ride instead?"

"Now?"

She laughed, then shook her head. "During the day."

"You do realize it's winter, right? Not really the best boating season."

"Will you take me out to catch some lobsters?" A smile grew on her face.

He waited to answer as a buzzing feeling swept over him. "Only if you wear a skipper outfit."

She laughed harder this time, her head tilted back. It was like an old song. Memories of the old days flooded his head. "How about tomorrow?"

"That sounds perfect."

He popped his door open and jumped out. He tried to make it to the other side before she opened hers, but she had already hopped out of the truck.

"I'll pick you up at nine."

As he walked her to the front door, she remarked about the driveway being plowed. He didn't tell her he had arranged for the guys to do it, even had the van cleaned off.

The closer they got to the door, the stronger the urge to get close to her became.

"So, tomorrow?" She turned the door handle and pushed it open.

"Dress warm."

She gave a quick wave as she stepped inside.

He walked away as coolly as possible, but floored it to his apartment the second he got in the truck. He was late for Christmas dinner. His mom was going to kill him.

CHAPTER 6

"So, you made it," his younger sister Lauren razzed him as soon as he shut the door. She sat on the couch and didn't look up, her thumbs typing away on her phone.

"I'm not that late." He checked the clock. Only an hour. He looked around the room. His father was sitting in his recliner, Jack in the kitchen. "Adam and Elizabeth aren't even here."

"We told them to come a little bit later." Jack handed him a beer. "We figured you'd be late, after carving the trails."

"Ha, ha." Matt twisted the cap off. "Speaking of which, where's your ball and chain?"

Jack rolled his eyes. "In the kitchen."

Matt looked in the kitchen and saw Rachael walking out of the pantry with his mom, the two of them fixing something together. Their relationship was natural and easy. Justine and Sarah were like oil and water. Never easy.

"Well, you decided to show up." Sarah didn't waste any time.

"I think it was very nice of you to take her snowboarding today," Rachael said, while laying napkins on the table.

"Yes, it was." Sarah nodded. "She must be devastated. Apparently, her fiancé hasn't called her since the whole thing happened."

"She was supposed to have a guy with her?" John asked from his chair.

"Seriously?" Lauren looked up from her phone. "Mom's been talking about this all day."

John just shrugged and returned to reading the paper.

Matt hated thinking about his reaction in the snowstorm. She came to Camden Cove alone. All alone. He looked out the window toward Vivi's house. He wanted to head over there and make sure she didn't spend Christmas evening alone, as well, but he decided against it. Tomorrow, he'd take her out on the water and do whatever it took to get her mind off the guy who was crazy enough to let her go.

Sarah shook her head. "Frank said she had no idea it was coming."

"Mom, stop," Matt said, as a sudden urge to protect her privacy came over him.

She put her hand on her chest and shook her head. "I just feel terrible for her."

"It's none of our business what happened." He knew how much the women loved a good story, but it didn't feel right, letting them talk about Katie.

Sarah looked to Rachael, then to Lauren.

The door swung open and his sister walked in with Lucy. Her husband Adam came in behind them with presents in his arms. Matt got up to help.

"Did you hear about Tyler?" Jack asked from the couch.

Matt had noticed that his cousin had called while he was out with Katie, but he figured he was calling for the holidays. "No, what?"

"Some of his traps were cut, too," Jack said. "Out by Taylor's Falls."

Two days of tampering with cages, two different families. This was no longer a joke. "Do they know who's doing this?"

Jack shook his head. "You should be careful." He leaned closer to Matt. "I heard Freddy's buddy O'Malley is back in town."

There were no laws protecting Maine's long history of territory rights, but the Atlantic fishermen almost always abided by unwritten rules like law. Families passed down territories from father to son.

Before he could say anything else on the matter, Lucy ran up and squeezed him into a big hug, squealing in delight.

"I thought the lady in the pretty dress was going to be here," Lucy said. "Is she your girlfriend?"

He noticed that the women in the room all became quiet. "No, she's not my girlfriend."

Jack turned to hang up the coats, then started in just as Matt predicted. "So you just take random women snowboarding?"

Matt looked at his mother as she hugged Lucy, ignoring him.

"You totally still have a thing for her," Elizabeth teased. "You were practically drooling last night."

He rolled his eyes. "I was not."

He hoped he hadn't been. Did Katie think that, too?

"He asked me to give back a mixed CD she made for him!" Lauren hooted from the couch. The women erupted into laughter.

"Last night, you two looked like you were having fun," Elizabeth continued tormenting him.

He didn't engage in any of the banter. It was all true, of course, but Matt wasn't going to admit it.

Kate sat in front of the fire with the lights out. Her phone lay face down on the floor in front of her, her journal next to it. She took another deep breath and held it in as she stared at the pulsating coals. Her thoughts swirled out of control once again.

Off in the distance, the ocean's symphony played its familiar tune. The night had not been as hard as expected. With the driveway and van cleaned off, it prompted her to take a long drive, winding along Route 1, playing sad love songs as she passed through the small seaside villages. When she made her way back home, she found leftovers from the night before with David and Frank, along with more chocolate truffles, in the fridge.

As she sat in front of the fire, she opened the leather cover of her journal and wrote *lobstering*. She immediately crossed it out. She didn't want to jinx herself. Planning didn't seem to work out that well for her.

And just like that, Eric popped into her head. Things she didn't allow herself to see before, that were now as clear as day. Problems she either denied, or chose to ignore. Not that it mattered now, she supposed, but her heart didn't seem to want to admit it. She still held out hope that they could be fixed, just as soon as he reached out to her. How long was she willing to wait?

The *what-ifs* took over. What if she hadn't pushed the dream wedding so much? What if they waited to buy a house? What if she paid attention to the signs?

A while back, a drive and an old love song used to help get her mind off her pain, but now her pain just remained there. Anchored.

CHAPTER 7

*E*very excuse popped into her head as to why she should stay in bed. It was dark out, for one. It was also cold and slippery, with the snow. Her swollen nose throbbed, and she couldn't breathe through it. She was alone.

When the excuses ran out, she swung her feet over the side of the bed and got up. It was completely dark out still, but she knew if she didn't do it in the morning, she'd never do it. So, she laced up her running shoes and peered out the window at the moon glowing behind feathery clouds. She'd push to get one mile done and go from there.

She pulled her hair into a tight ponytail and left her phone on the kitchen table. She always ran to music, but her phone had become a burden she no longer wanted to carry. Today, she'd take in the pulse of the ocean.

She started out slow. Her rhythm mimicked the crashing waves, but soon she gained her footing and fell into her regular tempo. Her feet created a soft beat against the packed snow.

The sidewalk had been cleared on Prospect Street, which ran perpendicular to Shoreview Drive. The lit steeple from the Congregational Church stood above the houses and to her left. The horseshoe shape of Camden Cove could be seen over the basin. The only lights on in the seaside village below were the Christmas tree and the bakery.

With each exhale, her breath billowed out in front of her, incandescent under the streetlights. The air felt humid, not bitter like in Minnesota. She loved running in the cold, especially early. Everything was still, a magnified quiet that only happened in the winter. Even the stars appeared brighter, the smells fresher.

After her second mile, she realized she hadn't been thinking about anything other than moving forward. By her fourth, her breath was in sync with her steps. One. Two. Three. Breathe.

By mile six, she had made it back to the village square and stopped along the harbor's railing. A buzz filled her body as she watched the boats' bows bob up and down in the water. The adrenaline from her run sent a warming sensation rushing over her.

Off on the horizon, the sun peeked out and the sky came alive. Sea smoke danced upon the surface of the water. Behind it, a pink streak contrasted against the ocean's black edge. She had seen that same pink streak the night before she left Perkins Cove that summer with Matt. They sat out on the swing of Vivi's screened porch as the sun set. That night, she wished nothing would ever change, but she had known even then, her real-life fairytale was about to come to an end.

Once back home, her parents' divorce made her realistic, even at sixteen. If her parents couldn't make it after twenty years, then a cross-country teenage relationship didn't have a chance.

Matt had called her for months. Then he wrote emails after she stopped calling back. He'd write about fishing, or how much he missed her. After a year, he wrote his last one. Asking if she was still coming out that summer. She never replied.

What if she'd called him back, instead? How long would they have dragged out the inevitable? His own divorce proved once again that happily-ever-afters were just fantasy.

The thought of starting over, beginning again, made her panic.

She didn't want to date again. Have her married friends set her up, like her sister. She inhaled a deep breath of salty air to bring her back to the present, then heard a bell jingling against glass.

"Good morning, Kate." She turned to see David standing in the doorway. Floury handprints smudged the front of his black apron with *La Patisserie* written in cursive font she didn't recognize. She guessed it had been a default font from a sewing machine. "Want to come in for a cup of coffee? On the house."

"That sounds wonderful." She wiped the sweaty wisps of hair from her face and began to cross the street, but suddenly stopped. "But I've just come from a run. I'm not really appropriate."

He scrutinized her as he approached. "What happened to your face?"

Her hand touched her swollen nose. She had forgotten about the purple tinge in the corners of her eyes. "I fell while snowboarding yesterday."

"I warned Matt not to get you hurt." He examined her more closely. "Did he skip the beginner lesson?"

"I didn't even make it off the bunny hill." She laughed as the image of Matt helping her down the mountain popped into her head, her panic dissipating.

"Well, come inside. You deserve a treat. I've just pulled out my mille-feuilles."

She didn't know what David said, but her stomach growled at the possibilities. He held the door open as she stepped inside.

A warm glow illuminated the room. Candle flames flickered in lanterns on each of the small, round tables. Three chandeliers were dimmed low, and their light reflected off the mirrored backing of the wooden shelves that held plates, bowls, and glasses, all neatly stacked.

"Have you opened?" Kate hadn't noticed a sign for store hours.

"In the winter, I open when someone shows up." He walked to

the coffee station and grabbed a mug. "How about our dark roast?"

"That would be great." The buzzing, warming sensation flowed back through her body again. She deserved none of the generosity she continued to receive.

"It must've been freezing." He filled the mug, looking out the window. "It's not even thirty degrees yet."

"It's peaceful," she explained, as he handed her the warm mug.

"Yes, I guess it is." He smiled and ushered her to a table by the counter. He pulled out a chair for her.

"When do you get here?" she asked as she sat down. She pulled off the headband that covered her ears. She could only imagine how ridiculous she looked, wiping the loose strands away from her face. "I saw the lights on when I left at five."

"This time of year, it depends on my mood, but I like the mornings. Luckily for me, my line of work requires early hours." He walked behind the counter and came back with a plate in his hand. "Tell me what you think."

A long, slender, sugared confection melted in her mouth. The light, airy pastry was delectable. She licked her fingers immediately. "Mmm..." she moaned. "What is this again?"

"Brioche beignet, but you've probably heard it referred to as a donut," he said.

"So this is a true patisserie, you're a master patissier."

"Well, as true as you can get outside of Paris." He sat across from her, resting his elbows on the table, watching her enjoy his treat.

"It's very welcoming in here." She admired all the decorations throughout the room. Twelve-foot oars hung on the wall. A wooden lobster trap, filled with burlap coffee bags, sat on top of the shelves. A collage of black and white photographs hung along a brick wall. The space felt oddly familiar and comfortable.

"That's all Frank." He gestured around the room. "He's goes all over to find some of these trinkets."

"Those are great photographs." Kate noticed that most of the photos were of Camden Cove.

David pointed toward a picture of a fisherman standing on a dock in front of a boat named *Sarah Marie*. "That's Matt's grandfather."

In the photograph, the man held a lobster the size of a cocker spaniel in both hands. A cigarette hung from the corner of his mouth. His face appeared serious, but his eyes gave away his pride. They looked like Matt's. "I've never seen such a big lobster."

"Legend has it that it was eighteen pounds."

Kate suddenly felt ashamed that she had left the Christmas party without saying goodbye. After all David and Frank had done for her, she didn't even bother to thank them. "I'm really sorry I snuck out of the party the other night. You both have been so kind to me."

"There's no need to apologize." David shook his head. "Now, come in the back and keep me company while I finish frosting Mrs. Johnson's birthday cake."

Kate looked around the empty space and hesitated. "Are you sure I'm not bothering you? I don't want to interrupt."

David waved his hand, dismissing her worries. "Come on. Bring your coffee."

Kate grabbed her brioche beignet and followed him through the swinging door. Her eyes immediately looked up to a tin ceiling. On one side of the room, two large commercial ovens sat next to metal shelves filled with pots and pans, trays and baskets of utensils. On the other side, glass fridges stood next to a large basin filled with dirty metal trays. A white marble island stood in the middle of the room, coated with flour. David motioned for her to sit at a stool next to it.

He topped off her coffee, then set the cream and sugar in front of her just as the oven buzzed. He pulled out a cookie sheet and placed it on the counter. With a metal spatula, he lifted triangular pastries, laid them on a linen covered tray, and slid one on a plate, shoving it across the island to her.

"What's this one?" Kate blew on the steam rising from the new flaky treat. Warm apple and cinnamon filled the air.

"It's called *chausson aux pommes*," he said, "or an apple turnover."

"What's your favorite type of dessert to bake?" she asked, wondering what a pastry chef most enjoyed.

He looked to the ceiling as he thought of his answer. "I love a wedding cake. The sheer decadence of it all makes for a lot of possibilities. I love creating flavors that leave your whole palette wanting more."

"Weddings must be a big part of your business." Kate waited for the emotional tidal wave to wash over her, but surprisingly it didn't.

"We do lots of weddings, mostly in the summer, and a lot in autumn." David arranged the pastries in straight, uniform lines. "Most of our business comes from the restaurants and hotels in the area. This was only a dream until I met Frank. Twenty years later, here we are."

Kate could see the pride on David's face. She couldn't help but feel a pang of jealousy. She had always dreamt of going out on her own and starting a design company. She wanted to start small, focus on local businesses at first, small projects and low budgets, but then expand by targeting bigger markets. At one time, she had even started putting money aside for start-up costs, but instead she used it for the down payment on her and Eric's house.

What would they do about the house?

She watched David as he grabbed a bowl of frosting from the fridge. He used a metal cake knife to stir in the teal coloring. Then he filled a frosting bag and began writing "Happy Birthday" on top.

"What happens next?" he asked. Kate looked up, suddenly realizing she had been staring off into the distance.

"What do you mean?" But she knew exactly what he meant. She wanted to stall to think of an answer, because even though she had been asking the same question since she stepped off the plane, she didn't have an answer.

She shrugged. But what *was* she going to do?

She wasn't going to stay at her and Eric's place. She could probably stay with her mom until she found something, but the idea of going back home made her sick. Moving back into her childhood bedroom at thirty-two years old was hitting rock bottom, and living with her sister and her happy family would be worse. And it all was soon to be her reality in less than a week. Her heart raced at the thought of it.

David studied her for a moment and said, "There's a French expression called *au pif*. It means "by the nose", or to cook by feel, and use your senses." David filled the frosting bag again, folding over the end when it was full. He squeezed it until a small amount of frosting piped out of the tip. "Sometimes we're so dependent on the recipe to tell us what to do, we go against our own gut feeling. What's your gut telling you?"

A few days ago, she couldn't wait to leave the seaside village, now she dreaded it. The worst part for Kate was that she didn't have a plan. And she always had a plan. Not having a plan freaked her out more than anything else. She lived by creating lists, organizing every detail of her life. The plan kept her safe.

But where did it get her? He left, anyway.

Maybe it was time she listened to her gut.

Then she heard a horn blow off in the distance.

And suddenly she said, "To go lobstering."

Matt checked the rearview mirror before he stepped out of the truck. A nervous energy ran through his body. He couldn't wait to be with Katie, especially after their day together on the mountain, but his sixteen-year-old insecure self kept sneaking to the surface.

Katie was sophisticated and way out of his league. But life didn't give second chances every day. He'd be a fool to not go for the catch, even if his chances were slim.

He rang the doorbell and waited for her to answer, playing out the day in his head. He'd take her up the coast. Simple was the key to making a cold fishing trip a success. He packed hot cocoa for a break, and clam chowder for lunch, with a fresh loaf of bread he grabbed from his uncle on the way.

When the door opened, all he saw was a figure standing in head-to-toe winter apparel. The only thing he could see of Katie was her eyes.

"Good morning!" she said through her scarf.

"You look fantastic." And he meant it. Even though he could only see a pair of black eyes, she looked as beautiful as she did in that fancy black dress on Christmas Eve. Then he wondered what she'd look like waking up next to him. He shook the thoughts away as she pulled down her scarf, and he noticed her cheeks flush as if she could read his mind.

She straightened her arms out from her sides. "I feel like the kid from The Christmas Story."

Matt tilted his head, taking a better look. "More like his brother Randy."

She laughed out, "Thanks."

"Ready to catch some lobsters?" He drawled out the letter R to exaggerate his New England accent.

"Wicked ready," she said, and it made him laugh. She picked up a bag sitting on the table, and hesitated before she grabbed her phone.

"Let's go, Minnesota."

After a second hesitation, she stuffed her phone in her jacket pocket.

Their conversation stayed light on the short ride down to the harbor. The sun peeking out of the clouds showed the promise of the day ahead. Usually during this time of year, Matt stayed off the water. The weather was unpredictable, dangerous even, but the forecast said clear skies for the day.

After he parked, he led her down to the floating dock. The path had barely been cleaned off, making them unsteady on their feet. He put his hand on the small of her back to help guide her. He could feel electric currents radiating from where he touched her, even through the goose feathers. How was he going to spend the day with her and keep his cool?

The low rumble of a diesel engine bellyached in the distance with the cacophony of seagulls up above.

Matt stopped once they reached the end of the floating boat ramp and pointed to a boat. "She's the one with the red hull, down there on the right."

Katie shielded the sun with her hand. "She's beautiful."

Matt could feel his pride swelling up. She was a boat to most people, but she signified everything he had worked for his whole life. And he loved that Katie saw her beauty, too.

He led her to his boat slip and held out his hand to help her onboard.

"Who's Maggie Mae?" She pointed to the name written on the stern of the boat as she climbed in.

"My family dog." He smelled the shampoo in her hair as she stepped past him.

He took a second before climbing on deck to compose himself. He needed to chill out, or he was going to freak her out, because he was freaking himself out. He was fooling himself about Katie. He had no business to get involved with someone right now. Justine had proved that. He needed to get his head out of the clouds.

Then he watched as she walked across the boat. She put her hands on the railing and looked out toward the water. The wind blew her hair across her cheek and she closed her eyes, lifting her head up to the sun.

He imagined pulling her into a kiss.

He must love complications.

When she turned back around, he began to busy himself, pulling off the five-gallon bucket from the exhaust pipe and unlocking the door to the wheelhouse. "Today, you'll be my sternwoman."

"What exactly does a sternwoman do?" she asked, stepping up beside him.

"Basically, you put the bait into the lobster pots." Matt pointed to the tank full of herring on the deck, fresh from the fishermen's pier earlier that morning. Then he turned to the dozen yellow traps sitting at the stern of the boat. "After that, we drop the pots into the water."

"What's the most important thing I should know?"

"Don't get caught in the rope." He opened the door and the tangy smell of salt and diesel fuel followed them inside the small standing space.

"What do you mean?" Katie asked, standing next to him. "What happens if I get caught in the rope?"

"You'll be swimming with the lobsters." He dragged out the *r* again, but the humor was lost on Katie. Her eyes opened wide. "You'll be fine, Minnesota." He handed over a pair of Grunden overalls. "Here's your outfit."

He began his ritual, flipping the battery switch and checking the fuel line before starting the engine. He turned up the volume on the marine radio and checked the dial to see if it was still set on channel four for weather. He knew it would be, but superstition made him follow the same routine. Everything in the same order. Besides, it never hurt to be extra cautious, especially with Katie on board.

She pulled on the bright orange rubber pants, which were ten sizes too big for her tiny stature, but somehow she managed to look great in them.

"Now you look like Ralphie."

"Hopefully you don't have to be limber to catch lobsters." She strapped the overalls on.

"Naw, just a little bit crazy."

Matt untied the bow line and moved to the stern, casting off from the dock. He returned to the wheel, reversing the boat out of its slip. Once clear, he throttled Maggie Mae forward at head speed until they cleared the no-wake zone. Even at the slow speed, the icy winter air swirled throughout the wheelhouse.

"Are you always alone when you fish?" she asked.

He shook his head. "In the summer, I usually have someone working with me. Last year, I had a guy all the way from Oxford," he spoke up over the engine. "He barely earned anything, but he has already asked me to come back next summer."

"I can see why," she said. "This is hard to beat, that's for sure. I've never stopped thinking about this place."

He almost asked why she never came back, but instead he steered Maggie Mae underneath the walking bridge and headed out toward the open waters.

Soon Camden Cove blended in with the other surroundings, its familiar landmarks fading into the landscape. Nothing but the rocky coast and ocean could be seen for miles. He couldn't hold back a smile as she gazed out the window of the wheelhouse. He knew the look all too well. The magic of the open ocean took hold of her.

"Thank you for doing this for me, and for yesterday," she said loudly over the engine.

He shook his head. "You don't have to thank me."

"I'm sure by now you've heard about everything."

Matt made a face, then shrugged. "I know a little."

Katie smiled. "You didn't feel sorry for the pathetic woman who cried in a minivan?"

"Well, maybe a little."

She bit her bottom lip, but he could see she was holding back a smile.

"What I really feel bad about is how you still don't have any sense of balance. We'll have to be extra careful. We don't want you falling overboard." This time she didn't hold back, she closed her eyes and laughed.

And, she looked happy.

He shook his head, and with a turn of the wheel, headed north. He couldn't help but wonder what kind of guy would leave a woman like Katie. Maybe if he had tried harder to keep her all those years ago, she would've come back like she promised. He shook his head, trying to break up his thoughts. He didn't have time for make-believe.

"We'll drop the first line up there." He pointed to one of his favorite spots, an inlet between Black Rock Island and Perkins Beach. He maneuvered the boat closer to the coast, but stayed a mile or so away from shore.

"During the summer, these coves are filled with buoys."

Matt's were painted a bright orange and blue. Each one had MMW in big bold capital letters printed vertically down the center. He had decided on the design when he was a kid.

"How do you know where to drop the lobster traps?"

"I've been fishing out here for over twenty years. I could tell you the depths by just looking out at the shoreline, but I use the machines to help me, too." Matt pointed to the fish finder, which not only provided the depth, but what fish were out there. "I mark the locations where I drop my lines." With one hand, he pushed the throttle forward while keeping the other on the wheel, and slowed to a stop. "We'll drop anchor here."

He put the engine in neutral and waves lapped against the boat as it rocked from side to side.

"So, this is what you do every day?" she asked, looking around the boat.

Matt didn't know how to read her. Was she not impressed? "Yeah, this is it."

She looked out at the water, took in a deep breath and said, "It's incredible."

He wanted so badly to reach out and tangle his fingers in her hair and kiss her, but he just nodded. "It doesn't get much better than this."

~

Kate wrapped her scarf around her neck a second time, covering her nose and mouth. Even inside the wheelhouse, the cold snuck in from behind, but it didn't stop the adrenaline from pumping through her body. She was at the helm of a lobster boat on the Atlantic Ocean.

The boat bobbed up and down in the water as the sun shone down on them.

He grabbed a pair of blue rubber gloves and handed them to her. "You ready?"

"Just tell me what to do."

An anxious smile spread across her face as he left the wheelhouse for the stern.

"I use herring for my bait." He grabbed a mesh bag and pulled the mouth open. He dunked his hand into a water tank, pulled out a handful of shiny, silvery fish, and stuffed them all inside. Then he closed the opening. "We'll put the bait inside each pot, and then drop them into the water."

He handed her a bag. She plunged her gloved hand into the slippery fish and managed to pull out only one at a time. The fish wouldn't stay in her hands, slipping through her fingers. By the time she stuffed one bag, Matt had finished four.

"We'll drop a dozen today." He counted out the remaining bags and handed her another one.

Kate couldn't help but pause to take in the scenery. Each time she looked up, Maine's coastline called out to her, begging her to stop and admire its beauty. It was one of the most beautiful sights she'd ever seen. Granite coastlines were softened by pines, their shadows covering the white snow. Seagulls screeched overhead, pulling her attention back to the bait, and she finished her second bag as Matt finished the rest.

He grabbed them all and moved to the back of the boat where the traps sat. She followed him and watched as he opened the top of one of the traps. "Just toss the bait inside and close. Pretty simple."

She took a bag and opened the trap, placing the bait where Matt placed his. Once they were done, he picked up a trap. "We drop them off the starboard side."

She grunted as she grabbed the trap next to his. It was heavier than she expected, and it took her by surprise, making her stumble a bit. Just as she gained her sea legs, a swell dipped the boat and tipped it to the side. She staggered back, dropping the trap. It crashed onto the deck as she reached out to grab hold of something. Matt caught her in his arms. Her gloved hands wrapped around his neck as his arms cradled her back. Their eyes locked, and they stayed together through another large wave, dipping as the boat floated up and down. He stood solid against the motion, holding onto her. As the boat steadied itself, he gently settled her back on her feet.

"They're heavier than they look," he said.

"Yeah, I guess so." The words barely came out. Like a photo evoking a long-lost memory, the look in his eyes brought back feelings she hadn't felt for years. Her mind became fuzzy and light, the air around her making her a bit tipsy, as though she were floating. What was getting into her?

He picked up the trap and rested it on the edge of the railing. "We'll drop one, and then move up a little before dropping another. It's not the best time of year for catching lobsters, so we'll have to soak them for a few days. I'll hold the line while you drop the pot."

"Okay." She held onto the metal trap with both hands as it balanced on the side of the railing. He grabbed the rope attached to the trap. As he threw the buoy overboard, he nodded at her and she pushed the trap into the water. It splashed down and bobbed for a moment before being swallowed up.

"You're now an official Maineiac," he said.

She liked the sound of that.

He pointed to the wheelhouse with his thumb. "Let's move up a little bit and drop another." As they walked back inside, he asked, "How about taking the wheel?"

"Me?" She couldn't believe he'd trust her with his boat. She certainly wouldn't trust herself with her own boat, at this point.

"Who else?" He gestured to the captain's wheel and let her step in front of him. She placed her hands on the wheel as he spoke into her ear. "Keep your eye on the compass." He pointed in front of the wheel at a round dial. "Keep the needle on the "N" for north."

She straightened her stance as Matt pushed the throttle and the boat moved forward. She took in a deep breath of the tangy air, squeezing her hands on the wheel.

"Let's go a little faster," he said. "You can take the throttle."

The boat sped up, chopping through the waters. For the first time in a long time, she didn't need to know what happened next. The need for control waned as she enjoyed watching the moment unfold before her. Her body quivered with exhilaration. She captained a boat on the Atlantic Ocean.

The rest of the day was a blur. It didn't take long to drop the rest of the pots. After each one, with Matt's help, she steered Maggie Mae up the coast with him close behind her. The thrill of each drop became stronger as she became more comfortable with what she was doing. After the last drop, Matt leaned against the side of the boat and folded his arms against his chest as Maggie Mae floated up and down in the water.

"Of all the people to pull out of the ditch," he said, fixing his cap to keep the sun from his eyes.

"I know, right?" She loosened her scarf, the winter air feeling warmer as they stayed still in the water.

Swirling above them, seagulls made shadows on the floor of the deck. The waves sparkled in the sun like millions of diamonds as far as she could see. White clouds billowed on the horizon as if they were sinking into the water. She had to imagine that even on the most miserable day, it beat her office.

"Do you love it?" She hoped he did.

Matt nodded. "It's something my ex-wife never understood. She didn't understand why I wanted to fish so badly. The weather is unpredictable and dangerous. The upkeep costs are expensive. The rules and regulations keep changing, and on and on." Matt's gaze focused out on the water. "She was right, of course." Then he focused on her. "But there's no way I wanted to work inside all day, waiting to get out here. It's not just a job for me. It's my life."

Matt's eyes were thoughtful, but intense. She wondered if she felt so passionately about anything in her life. Willing to lose everything for it.

"I always thought I'd love my job." Kate shrugged. Her voice lacked any of the enthusiasm Matt's had. She thought of the design firm. It was everything she had wanted in a career, but now, she wanted something else. Something more. "But it's just a job."

And the only thing she could count on in her life. How terribly depressing.

"I remember what an amazing artist you were back then."

Matt couldn't possibly remember her silly drawings and paintings, could he? She couldn't remember the last time she had picked up her sketch pad, or did anything creative for that matter.

"What's he like?" he asked, snapping her out of her thoughts when she realized he was talking to her. "You don't have to answer that."

He must've mistaken her confusion.

"Who? Eric?" She pulled back a loose strand of hair and tucked it behind her ear. It had been days since she had seen or spoken to him. The longest amount of time they'd been apart since they were first together. She missed him. And she wished with everything she had, that she didn't miss him, because getting on with life would be so much easier.

"Smart. Ambitious. He's a gentleman. He's cautious." She blew out. "He comes from a really great family."

She stood up straighter, feeling her shoulders tense up. All morning, she had been avoiding the thought of Eric.

"I'm sorry." Matt held up his hands. "It's none of my business."

"No, it's not that." The truth was, she had to face the fact that Eric was now just a memory. Her love story had turned out to be a fake. For all she knew, he had moved on, found someone else, or was happy to be on his own. He was no longer hers. "We were together almost five years. He's a lot like me. Plans everything out. Doesn't like risks. He'd never go fishing."

Matt smirked.

Kate focused on the horizon before admitting the truth. "I think I probably bored him."

Matt straightened up, his eyes digging into hers. "You're the furthest thing from boring."

Kate's cheeks warmed, even in the chill of the winter's day.

The day before her treasure hunt of sea glass, Matt had stolen her attention. They had been at church, and in the quiet of a service, when the congregation was listening to the minister, she noticed the cute boy from Maine. Even though most people were dressed in their Sunday best, Matt wore shorts and flip-flops, with a Red Sox cap tucked underneath his arm. Then, from the middle of his hymnal, he pulled up a comic book and read during the service. He was the only kid Vivi ever excused for bad behavior in church.

"As long as he sits and is respectful, there's no harm in letting the boy read," Vivi had said, when Kate questioned his actions. "Sarah and John have done a fine job with their children."

But it wasn't until she was sixteen, the summer she came out alone, one afternoon, on one of her walks home from the library, he pulled his car over to the sidewalk and offered her a ride home. When he dropped her off, he asked her to go surfing.

She couldn't believe a guy like Matt wanted to spend time with her. He had total confidence. He didn't even hesitate when he asked her out. He probably knew she'd say yes. And standing here on the boat with him, she could still feel that magnetism. It was hard not to admire his self-assurance and carefree personality.

But truth be told, the teenage relationship was a stroke of luck. Back home, a Matt Williams would've been unattainable for a girl like Kate. He was adventurous, exciting, and outgoing. She was shy, cautious, and a book worm. He never had the chance to figure out, that summer, that she wasn't anything close to exciting or adventurous.

She lived safe. That's why she and Eric were so compatible. He was cautious, careful, and level-headed. He didn't believe in fate.

Off along the horizon, clouds rolled across its surface, coming closer. It looked as though they would soon surround the boat. "Is that a storm approaching?"

"That's a snow squall." Matt didn't appear worried about the change in weather. "It'll probably pass as quickly as it comes." Matt pushed himself off the railing. "But we should probably head back, anyhow."

Kate nodded, but wished they could stay out on the water forever. As the engine rumbled, she moved to the stern of the boat. Even with the squall brewing off in the distance, the waves were as calm as she felt inside. Not once had she thought about life while she hauled those traps. That was the mystique of lobstering. She was dragged into the process like the water dragging the traps down.

As she became hypnotized by the sea, a vibration snapped her back to reality. Her phone pulsated in her coat pocket. She lost the rhythm of her breath and the creeping warmth of anxiety brewed in her legs, climbing up to her chest. The familiar noose wrapped itself around her ribcage and began to tighten. The phone continued to pulse. She struggled with what to do. She didn't want to know who was on the other end. Matt stood in the wheelhouse, his attention on the shoreline ahead. Not a worry on his mind.

Her phone stopped, and her heart slowed down. She took a breath, but the pulsation started right back up again. Before she could regret it, she pulled the phone from her pocket, and without looking, threw it as far into the ocean as she could. She didn't want to know who was calling her anymore. She needed to stop worrying and compulsively thinking *when* or *why not*. She needed to dump her old life in the ocean, just like the lobster pots, and start over.

CHAPTER 8

*E*lizabeth ate leftover Christmas dinner as she watched television from her parents' kitchen island. Her dad read in his chair. That was his happy place, reading in front of a whispering fire with their dog, Maggie Mae. He read a Tom Clancy novel. Ms. Lisa, Camden Cove's librarian, always put together a bundle for him at this time of year.

Her thoughts kept going back to Matt as her mom walked through the kitchen door.

"Well, isn't this a nice surprise," Sarah said. "What are you doing here?"

"I thought I'd stop by and say hi." Elizabeth leaned over the counter to kiss her mother on the cheek. "I just finished a surgery with Mrs. Wilson's dog, and I have a teeth cleaning this afternoon. I didn't want to drive all the way home and back."

Elizabeth set her plate on the counter, then looked back inside the fridge. "Don't you have more leftovers?"

Sarah pulled out containers from the fridge. "Have you talked to Lauren about last night?"

Elizabeth shook her head, but wondered if Sarah was thinking the same thing she was. Lauren came home late last night. She met up with Kyle, her on-again, off-again boyfriend, after Christmas dinner. Elizabeth hated the idea of Lauren being involved with a Harrington. Especially now, with Justine's engagement, not to mention everything with the divorce, she didn't understand why Lauren got herself involved.

"Where is Lauren?"

"Sleeping."

Elizabeth could tell that Sarah was trying everything she could to bite her tongue, but she couldn't hold it in any longer.

"She was out last night until one in the morning."

"Mom." Elizabeth's tone was stern. "Stay out of it. Kyle is not Freddy, and it's not like Lauren and Justine are swapping recipes."

"Her relationship with Kyle changes like the wind."

"Mom." Her tone was stern. "You really need to let this one go."

"But with Matt dealing with the divorce…"

"Mom."

"I just worry that she's—"

"Don't get involved." Elizabeth wasn't going to talk about it.

Sarah tapped her fingernails against the counter, trying hard to hold in the rest of what she wanted to say. She changed the subject. "Frank called this morning. Apparently, Matt took Kate O'Neil out on his boat."

Elizabeth smiled. Kate being back in town after all this time was incredible. It was either the best timing, or the worst. "Today? He's with her again?"

Sarah shrugged. She seemed pleased that Elizabeth wasn't scolding her about this new topic. "Matt agreed to take her out."

Elizabeth contemplated the news for a moment. "I hope this doesn't end up like the last time she left."

Elizabeth had forgotten about Matt moping around the house. For months he waited by the phone for her to call. "Luckily, he's no longer a teenager."

"I don't know," Elizabeth said, taking a bite of cold lobster claw. "The way he was looking at her the other night reminded me of the sixteen-year-old Matt."

Sarah waved her hand dismissively at Elizabeth, but she knew she was pretending. Frank agreed that Matt appeared happier the past few days, since Kate arrived.

"Whatever makes him happy," Sarah said.

Elizabeth gave her a look.

"What?"

"Don't." Elizabeth could tell her warning meant nothing to her mother.

"What do you mean?"

Elizabeth dug her fork into more mac 'n cheese. "Please, don't start meddling in this. Whatever it is."

Sarah placed a hand on her chest. "Me? Meddle?"

"Ha!" hooted John, from the other side of the room. This made Elizabeth snicker as well.

"What are you two laughing at?" Sarah huffed. John began to cough. "I'm not going to meddle in Matt's love life. I swear, the two of you are being ridiculous."

She picked up her mug and walked out of the room. Elizabeth guessed she was going to call Frank.

Something happened to Katie on the boat. Matt could tell by the way she was leaning against the washboard. She stood up straight, her shoulders back, her chin held high. Her hair blew back away from her face. She seemed to be at ease, not troubled like the days before. The water worked wonders that way.

When he first thought about taking her snowboarding, he did feel sorry for her. Here she was, all alone on Christmas. She still had the ring, so she wasn't sure whether her engagement was completely off.

Now her ring finger was bare.

He also understood. He had been there. He had survived a very public break up. He knew how lonely and terrible it felt. Justine ripped his heart apart then stomped on it with Freddy.

At one point, he may have fooled himself that Katie was an old friend in need. A smart, beautiful friend, and not feel anything more. He knew neither one of them was in a position to get involved in a relationship. Not to mention that she lived across the country. But the more time he spent with her, the more she was on his mind. If he was honest with himself, he wasn't sure if he had ever stopped thinking about her. She had always been the girl that got away, and he hated the idea of her slipping away again. Whatever happened between her and her fiancé was none of his business. But it was hard to know that she was single, while also knowing her heart was with someone else.

The summer with Katie was one of the best in his life. He had wanted things to work out between them so badly, but when life returned to normal and the summer heat disappeared like the leaves on the trees, she called him less and less. He wasn't necessarily surprised when she stopped altogether.

That's when Justine came into the picture.

Justine had always been the girl next door. A Camden Cove native like himself, Justine grew up on the harbor, at the beach, and was also from a family of local business owners. She was like her parents, his parents, and their parents before that. They both stuck around town after graduation, living at home. Justine commuted to Portland for school while Matt worked as a sternman on his grandfather's boat during the day and cooked in the restaurant at night. It seemed they were a couple before he even realized what was happening.

When they started dating, he had just started fishing full-time. At first, Matt could handle the schedule—waking up before four, out on the water for at least eight hours, then another eight at the restaurant. Justine seemed to understand in the beginning, but when his schedule didn't change while he waited for his license, she became less so. He couldn't blame her. He could only give her a night or two a week, and on those nights he was exhausted.

They dated on and off through the years, but once she graduated, Justine started talking about marriage. To say that Matt wasn't ready, was an understatement. He was still living under his parents' roof. He only earned twenty percent of the daily catch as a sternman, and anything he made as a line cook, he stored away for his own boat. There was no way he could afford it, plus he wasn't ready to be a husband. He wanted to go out with the boys, not settle down and play house.

"Why don't you just work at the restaurant like Jack?" Justine would often ask. "Why do you have to fish?"

That was the first sign they were wrong for each other. Justine never liked the idea of him trying to get his own boat and crew. If he could have a job that was certain, in his family's business, a restaurant that had been successful for years, why struggle in fishery? When Matt tried to explain how working on the water was a part of him and made him happy, Justine couldn't understand.

The second thing wrong about them was Freddy Harrington.

Freddy was always on the fringes. Whenever they got into an argument, Freddy was there waiting, ready to swoop in and lend an ear or a shoulder to cry on.

Somehow Freddy managed to get a license from the state, a boat from his dad, and packed the area with his traps everywhere, including Matt's family's territory.

The third problem was that Justine got pregnant.

The fourth... they got married.

They didn't even get engaged. They just eloped, driving down to city hall, a woman paying her dog's license their witness. Soon, she became resentful of him working all the time. She wanted to try for another baby, and he didn't even want to consider it. Their tiny two-bedroom house became smaller as time went on. One night, after a double shift, he found Justine crying at the kitchen table.

"I want a husband."

"You *have* a husband." Annoyance rang in his voice. Did she think he liked working all day and night?

"Do you even know where I was last night?"

Matt looked at her and realized he didn't. He had come home and gone straight to bed after his shift. He figured she was out with friends.

"A normal couple checks in, but you never do." Justine stopped making eye contact. "I'm like a roommate."

If he had known Freddy was behind the scenes, lurking in the shadows, waiting for the right moment to sneak in, Matt might have worked harder on fixing things between them. He was just so tired all the time. He hadn't really noticed her feelings. Life was hard, but wasn't that the point of being married, sticking with it through the tough times?

He didn't know how bad it was until it was too late. He and Justine had been fighting a lot, but he figured it was a mixture of everything.

It was Sarah who noticed Justine's bracelet, gold, with a small charm dangling from her wrist. Matt wouldn't have thought anything of it, but Sarah asked if he had given it to Justine.

Justine had straightened up, but pulled her shirtsleeve down to cover the piece of jewelry. "A friend gave it to me."

"That's an awfully nice friend." Sarah's tone was harsh, and Matt was annoyed that his mother had been so rude. He was going to say something, but something about the way Justine held her stare with Sarah made him hesitate. For the rest of the night, Justine hid the bracelet. When she went to bed, she kept it on as she slept. Once he knew she was asleep, he studied it.

The charm was of an anchor. Anyone would have thought it was from Matt.

He knew it was from Freddy.

What Matt never understood, even to this day, was why she just didn't have enough guts to come out and tell him. She just dangled it out there like bait, waiting for him to discover it. Or his brother Jack, considering he was the one who walked in on her and Freddy above the restaurant.

The female Williamses cursed Justine when she moved

Freddy directly into their house. Luckily the divorce was quick, and Matt heard that Freddy covered Justine's lawyer's fees.

He figured that's how life worked. Just when he hit rock bottom, something brought him back to the surface, so he could breathe again. And now, as he watched Katie standing there on the boat, he knew that life was giving him another shot. As he pulled into the harbor, watching the shoreline come into focus, he knew he'd be a fool to let her go again.

Once he docked Maggie Mae into her slip, he closed everything up and they walked down the dock together.

"Want to grab a coffee?" she asked. "My treat."

"Absolutely."

Maybe it was the energy from the sea or being around Katie again, but he didn't want their day to end. They talked as they crossed Harbor Lane, then Matt suddenly stopped in the middle of the street.

"What is my mother doing?" he said, looking inside the bakery. Sitting at the window with Frank and David, Sarah waved.

"They're up to something," he said, stepping up onto the sidewalk and opening the door for her.

"What do you mean, they're up to something?" she asked as they walked inside.

"How was the boat ride?!" all three asked in unison.

Matt smirked as he said, "What a coincidence that you're all here."

Matt saw his mom give Frank a nod, and as if reading from a script, Frank asked Katie, "How about a cup of coffee?"

Sarah then proceeded with her part. "Why don't you two join us?"

Sarah gestured Matt and Katie to the two empty chairs that faced the harbor. She made a point to make eye contact with only Katie, because she knew that he knew what she was up to. Just as Matt was about to tease her, David slammed open the kitchen door with a plate of pastries in his hands.

"Would you like to sample some of my buttery madeleines?" David pushed the plate closest to Matt and Katie. "I dipped them in chocolate ganache."

Frank nonchalantly said, "Matt, I forgot I have a doctor's appointment tomorrow morning. I won't be able to do the delivery down to Boston. Do you mind going alone?"

Matt shook his head. "No problem, I can go myself."

Sarah asked Katie, "Have you ever been to Quincy Market?"

Katie finished chewing before she answered. "No, I've never been to Boston, other than the airport."

"It's lovely this time of year." Frank sounded casual, but Matt saw right through their act. "All the Christmas decorations and lights, and shopping around Faneuil Hall."

"The North End has so many great restaurants, and it's all right there," David said.

Matt almost choked on his coffee, but smiled when Katie raised her eyebrow at him not in on the ruse.

Undeterred, Frank soldiered on and suggested, "You should go down with Matt tomorrow. He'll show you around."

Matt was amused by their instigating. Then, just as they hoped, he fell into step. "You should come with me. I can take you around the city."

Everyone turned their attention to Katie. She thought for a moment, making Matt slowly die inside, thinking she was going to say no.

"I have no plans. That sounds wonderful."

Matt let out his held breath, hoping she didn't hear. A single laugh escaped Sarah as Frank practically jumped out of his seat. He tried to cover his enthusiasm by grabbing the plates and rushing back to the kitchen. David continued to suggest places to visit. "You need to see the harbor, and stop in at Haymarket, then hit the commons..."

∾

A cup of coffee and four pastries later, Kate walked with Matt down Harbor Lane to his truck.

"You do realize that was a set-up, don't you?" He pointed back toward the bakery with his thumb.

Kate looked back. Sarah, Frank, and David all waved through the window, still watching them. She laughed. "I didn't until now." She paused then said, "Oh... you don't have to take me."

"Are you kidding?" Matt stuffed his hands into his pockets. "I'm looking forward to it."

He pointed to the second-floor windows of The Fish Market. "That's my place, above the restaurant."

The Fish Market sat at the mouth of the cove, overlooking the granite shore. She covered her eyes with her hand and studied it. "That's an amazing view."

"It's cozy." He looked at the building. "It's perfect for me."

Emotions suddenly bubbled up inside her. Matt lived exactly the way he said he would all those years ago. The way he had always dreamed. Out on the ocean, in control of his own boat, his own business, his own life.

When did she stop believing in her dreams?

Worse, when did she stop believing in *herself*?

Eric leaving her didn't mean her life was over. Her mother's life may have fallen apart when her father left, but that didn't mean hers had to, as well.

Kate slowed at the end of the footbridge. "I think I'd like to walk back, if you don't mind."

He shook his head and pulled his hood up. "See you tomorrow?"

"Can't wait." Then she added, "Meet at the bakery?"

He nodded and walked backwards, calling out, "Nine o'clock."

The sun was setting as she arrived at Vivi's. Streaks of pink and lavender met the ocean's black edge. As she stepped inside, she looked for her phone, then remembered it plunging to the bottom of the ocean. She immediately regretted it.

What if Eric had been the one who was calling? What if he was trying to get in touch with her?

Vivi's home phone rang.

She ran to it and picked it up. "Hello?"

She held her breath until her sister Jen said, "Where have you been all day?"

Kate sat down on a kitchen stool and sighed audibly into the phone.

"Nice to hear from you, too." Her sister's tone sounded annoyed.

Kate rubbed her forehead. "No, it is, I'm sorry. I just thought you might be Eric."

Then it all came together. Jen was the one who had been calling her on the boat. The little hope she held out now faded away entirely. If he hadn't even bothered to text Merry Christmas back to her, then he wasn't ever going to reach out.

She listened to her sister, who talked about Christmas and her family. She listened, but looked out at the harbor and the lights on above The Fish Market. After her sister started to complain about being so busy with her family, Kate said, "I got to go, Jen."

She hung up the phone and looked out the windows at the golden lights above the restaurant. Being at the helm of that boat had been the best thing she's felt since leaving Minnesota. She'd give anything to be able to live life at the helm. Go after what she wanted, and not sit around feeling sorry for herself.

She didn't need Eric.

She needed to dream again.

CHAPTER 9

*K*ate woke with her journal lying on the other side of the bed, her computer screen opened and dead next to it. She must've fallen asleep at some point while she rested her eyes. Turning on her side, she peeked out the window. The sun's rays blended like watercolors across the sky, deep purples melting into pink and finally baby blue. In the pale dawn light, she could see the tiny village square. She grabbed her journal and looked over her new list.

Her list to start over, and start living.

She stretched and got out of bed, then threw on her robe. She wedged her feet into slippers and headed downstairs. As she cracked open the sliding glass door, the crashing of waves immediately surrounded her.

The air felt mild and a little humid. Perfect for running.

She looked in the direction of The Fish Market and noticed she was getting into that habit, especially now that she knew Matt lived there.

Thoughts of yesterday slipped in as she ate toast with peanut butter. Her goal was to run along the ocean's frozen shore.

Next was Quincy Market.

Then, eating in the North End.

And then hauling lobsters.

All in that order.

While she ran, she focused on another one of her lists. Her plans for when she returned to Minnesota. The first thing she had to do was move her things out of the house. The house was from another life, and she no longer wanted it. Eric hadn't moved in yet, but the space was too big for just her. Hopefully the sale would happen quickly, and whatever came from it, she would save. All of it would go toward start-up costs for her new business venture—Kate O'Neil Design.

Until she found a new place, she'd ask to stay with her mother, she couldn't stay there. She found a couple of listings in the city and enquired by emailing the real estate agents. The idea of owning her own business brought a new excitement she hadn't felt before. Throughout the night, she worked on her mission statement and her personal brand. She researched what she could online about business start-ups. She found advice about what she needed to do before setting out on her own, the initial costs and fees, whether or not to hire an attorney for filing for a LLC, and the costs of outsourcing assistance from independent contractors.

By the time Kate reached the beach, she realized she didn't want to wait. When she'd return to work, she'd hand in her notice.

She had worked in the industry for more than a decade, and had an extensive client list and more than a few who would recommend her work. She had kept detailed notes on all her accounts, and had a good rapport with her clients. For the first time in years, she could feel her dreams at her fingertips.

By the time Kate reached the end of Perkins Beach, gray clouds covered the sun's rays, but the snow still glowed against the dark granite bluffs. She stopped running and stood at the edge of the water, listening to the waves. Their roar against the rocky shores could be heard off in the distance, and had such an effect on her whole being. A day ago, she had felt the weight of the world on her shoulders. Now, as she stood at the mouth of the Atlantic she felt light, like a feather floating in the wind.

$$\sim$$

Matt listened as the meteorologist warned of a new nor'easter threatening to dump another twelve to eighteen inches on the East Coast. The unpredictability of these storms was usually what excited Matt the most, but the impending storm posed a problem for his and Katie's day in the city.

"This is going to be another big one, folks, so make sure you have extra food and water on hand. It's always good to have a battery-powered radio in case of a power outage."

He grabbed his phone and wallet before heading out the door, hoping she wouldn't cancel because of the snow. When he stepped inside the bakery, the crowd was a bit heavier than normal. He looked around, searching out Katie, reminded him that he needed to finally get her number.

"Did you hear about the storm coming in?" Frank asked as he got to the front of the line.

"I can't believe another nor'easter." They had been nailed this winter already, and it wasn't even January. They had at least four more months to go.

"I'm afraid so." Frank handed over a coffee cup. "You need to stock up on batteries, being up there above the restaurant!"

Frank mumbled something about retiring in Florida just as Katie walked in the door. Her eyes immediately sought his. She twisted her auburn curls and looked even more amazing.

"Well, hello!" Frank sang out.

Katie greeted Frank like a long lost friend.

From underneath the counter, Frank pulled out a basket of goodies. Matt shouldn't have been surprised that his uncles included pastries in their plans.

"A wicker basket?"

"What?" Frank asked, handing a set of keys to Matt. "The van's packed and ready to go. You two should be careful, and leave the city before the storm comes in."

She looked inside the bag. "These smell delicious."

Frank handed her a to-go cup. "Now grab some coffee before you leave."

Kate couldn't stable her breath as Matt's green eyes locked onto hers. Maybe it was seeing him in his element the day before, or maybe it was because his aftershave smelled so good, but she felt herself blush. He looked good. Real good.

He dressed casual, with a winter vest over a wool sweater and a pair of jeans just worn enough to fit him perfectly. But it wasn't what he was wearing that drew her in. It was the way he looked at her when she walked through the doors, as though she was the only person in the whole universe.

The room quickly warmed around her as he moved closer and said, "Good morning." His voice sounded like velvet.

"Good morning." The butterflies in her stomach made her quickly look away. She hoped he hadn't noticed the reddening of her face. She took a drink from her cup full of breakfast blend, and scorched the roof of her mouth.

Now she was creating fantasies with her old teenage crush, who was clearly just a nice guy. He didn't ask her to go to Quincy Market. It was a set-up. Her desperation must be palpable.

"Your eyes match your coat," he teased.

She looked down at her purple parka. "Well, I was finally able to breathe a little out of my nose this morning, which is a huge improvement." She had almost forgotten about her black eyes. She had put on concealer, but washed it off again. It had just made her look ill, instead of like she'd been knocked out by a bunny hill. She opted for only a little blush and mascara. "There's a big storm coming."

Matt nodded as he checked the weather on his phone. "We

should be able to spend most of the day in the city before it's supposed to start coming down."

"Did you order all this breakfast?" She lifted the basket up into the air, feeling the weight of its contents.

"That's just what my uncles do." Matt put his phone in his front jeans pocket. "I wanted to text you not to eat, but realized I didn't have your number."

She knew she would have to explain what happened to her phone, but she didn't want to have to tell why it was floating with the lobsters. "I got rid of it."

He slanted his head and squinted his eyes. "You're one interesting woman, Katie O'Neil."

Her shoulders immediately relaxed when he didn't pursue it further. Instead, he led her out of the shop to the white van that was parked along the sidewalk. She immediately recognized the Vivaldi font on the sliding doors that read La Patisserie. She would have gone with Bickham Script Pro instead, it was more Frank and David's style.

He opened the passenger door for her, then jogged around to the driver's side. Once she buckled her seat belt, she said, "You fish for lobsters, tow out stranded drivers, and deliver pastries. What don't you do?"

Matt turned the keys in the ignition. "I don't fly."

"At all? Or you just don't like to fly?"

"Both."

"I guess that's why you never came out to Minnesota."

"Well, not exactly." He looked as though he was going to say something else, but stopped himself. The mood immediately shifted, and she wished she hadn't said anything. She didn't want to rehash the past, because she knew she was the one who had been the scoundrel. Instead, she wanted to go to the city and live in the present.

He reached over to the radio and turned it up. The slow introduction to Sweet Caroline began playing. "You ready for Boston?"

She looked out the windshield at the road before them, and while taking in Neil Diamond's voice on the radio, she nodded. "Yes, I am."

"Let's go!"

They traveled along Route 1, wandering through small seaside villages until they hit New Hampshire, passing over Portsmouth's brick skyline covered in snow. The highway became crowded once they passed over the Massachusetts border. She leaned forward in her seat to see landmarks she remembered as a kid. Bunker Hill stood over triple-deckers, tree-lined neighborhoods edged the city's tallest buildings, and the harbor's docks were filled with ships and barges that ran along the edge of city. She swiveled around to get a good look at Zakim Bridge floating through the Boston.

The highway soon dipped underground, and the screech of wheels and brakes filled a dingy tunnel. Matt turned off onto an exit and the van climbed toward light. Soon the city embraced them. They were in the heart of Boston. Historic brick-and-mortar buildings sat in between tall, sleek skyscrapers.

Matt drove through the city's narrow streets, going down one-ways and taking sharp turns with ease. With one shot, he parallel parked next to a long brick building. "We just have to deliver to a few vendors, and then we'll hit up all the tourist spots."

He jumped out and opened the back doors, pulling out a cart. He began filling it with white boxes with *La Patisserie* written on top. She noticed the bakery's logo was in a different font than what was on the van, and both were different from their website's logo. This was only the kind of detail a designer would notice, she guessed, but it made their brand inconsistent. To advertise and market their business, they needed consistency, especially a small company that needed as much recognition as possible. An inconsistent brand could potentially confuse the buyer. Unfortunately, it didn't surprise her, either. Even with their professionalism and clear style, Frank and David couldn't afford a marketing team like the big corporations she designed for. You spent the money where you could.

Matt moved efficiently, and she knew he wouldn't accept it, but she asked anyway. "Do you need help?"

"Nah," he smiled at her. "After we finish the deliveries, you just tell me where you'd like to go."

"I have a craving for some Italian," she said, thinking of some of the North End restaurants she had looked up online last night.

That was when she'd taken a peek at Frank and David's website. They used a simple design, but if they were her clients, she'd showcase what she loved most about them—their unique take on a French patisserie. Their website felt flat, the pictures dull, and none of it showed Frank or David's personalities.

"There are plenty of places just up the road." Matt pointed to a long rectangular building the size of the whole block, with a gold dome in the middle. Four granite pillars flanked the entrance, with steps the width of the building. The gray granite building stood like a Bostonian Parthenon. Christmas garland wrapped the stone pillars. A decorated tree twinkled out on the cobblestone courtyard. It was a Christmas wonderland. "We'll hit Quincy Market first, and then Faneuil Hall."

Matt pushed the cart along the sidewalk, snow packed between the cobblestones. Snowbanks were piled everywhere, but even in the cold, vendors set up shop outside the marketplace.

They entered a glass structure, that reminded her of a greenhouse, warm and bright, but instead of plants and flowers, it was filled with bull carts selling touristy stuff like t-shirts, small trinkets and souvenirs. Matt led her up the ramp into the interior of the market. A quiet buzz filled the long hallway of food stalls ran down the middle of the building. Steam rose from behind glass walls. People stood in long lines waiting for every type of food imaginable: seafood, Italian, Indian, Asian, Middle-Eastern, coffee, ice cream, and more delicacies than she could count.

"This place used to be a fish and meat market." He pointed to the mammoth wooden signs against a brick wall. Standing tables filled the room, crammed with people enjoying the food. Up above, a circular railing opened to a second floor. She peered through the large rotunda, at least a few stories tall. The rotunda's space was massive, yet it felt warm and inviting with the light coming in and hitting the red brick walls, casting a warm glow throughout the space. The dome had been painted a creamy New England yellow with a pale blue railing opening up the second floor. Birds swooped from one side to the other. As they walked down the long hall of vendors, businessmen and women stood in line with college students and tourists for food. The energy of the space hummed off the walls.

"Let me stop at a couple vendors while you check the place out," Matt said, already starting down the hall. "Tell Mario at The Brew that your cappuccino is on me."

"Where should I meet you?" She didn't want to make him wait, or worse, get lost in the city.

"Don't worry. I'll find you." Matt waved as he took off down the corridor, disappearing into the crowd.

The space bustled around her. People weaved in and out of the lines in front the various vendors. The movement created an energy she enjoyed, but she didn't follow suit. Instead, she meandered along, checking out each stall. The scents melded into one. Spices melted into savory blending into sweet. She stopped for a cappuccino and thanked Mario with a very generous tip, then followed the long, tiled, passage.

She spotted Matt up ahead. He shook hands with a man and a woman, and they all talked with ease. A sudden pride grew inside her chest as she watched him pass over boxes of pastries. David and Frank had really created an amazing product. With David's mastery of pastries and Frank's chic style, they really had something that she felt would thrive, even beyond New England.

Then it hit her. She could help them. She could create a new, more modern website for La Patisserie. All she had to do was take some photos of David baking, with Frank's style showcased, and create a website that reflected their personalities. Then she could find the right market for their advertising to drum up more business. David would need to update anyways, as he was starting his new cooking classes. It could also be her way of thanking them.

She walked over to Matt and the vendors and asked, "Do you mind if I take some pictures of you for Frank and David?"

"Not at all."

As Matt delivered pastries, Kate took photos from different angles, hoping to capture the energy in the market and restaurants. The fluorescent lights weren't optimal, but she was able to catch enough backlight to show texture in the photos. Once Matt finished all the deliveries, they returned to the van with the empty cart and stowed it in the back. When he shut the doors, he grabbed her hand and started pulling her down the street. "Come on, we're going on a trolley ride."

"What?" She followed after him as he headed down the sidewalk.

"The duck ride would be too cold this time of year."

Every once in a while, he'd place his hand on the small of her back as they walked down the street. Each time, his touch sent an electrical current pulsating through her. When they reached the trolley, he waited until she boarded before climbing in. She picked a seat in front, next to the window. He sat down and leaned close. The leathery musk of his aftershave infused the air around her. As he looked out the window, pointing out landmarks before the tour guide did, he moved closer, his leg resting against hers. And suddenly, she wanted him to move even closer.

She wondered if her broken heart was twisting Matt's genuine kindness into something it was not. He had that natural ability to put everyone at ease when talking to him. She tried to ignore his touch on her leg.

After the tour through the city and a late lunch in the North End, the snow began to fall as they made their way back to the van.

"We should probably head back," Matt said as they walked along the cobblestone sidewalk.

She nodded, but secretly wished they could stay in the city forever. The day had been perfect, and she didn't want it to come to an end.

"I heard there's this bar where everyone knows your name." He said it so casually, she wasn't sure if he was serious or being silly.

"I hear people are always glad you came." As she spoke, his smile grew.

"I hear Boston's really something in a snowstorm."

"Yes, I've only heard, never been able to actually experience it."

He pulled out his phone and put it up to his ear. "Yes, hello," he said into it. He walked away, so she couldn't hear what he was saying.

Then he swung back around, stuffing his phone into his pocket. "You wouldn't believe it, but two rooms just happened to be available at the Harbor Hotel."

He was right. She couldn't believe it. "That sounds perfect."

They parked the van and walked around the city as the snow fell down around them. The whole time, they talked. They talked about everything. She told him about her parents' divorce, and he told her about his. She told him about her father's family, and about living at home during college. He told her about fishing, and cooking at the restaurant, and finally getting his own boat.

Then, she confessed the one secret that she had told no one. She told him about Kate O'Neil Designs. And like a faucet opening up, all of her ideas spilled out. Her ideas for Frank and David's website, the different ways she wanted to showcase not only David's work, but also their brand and style. She had told Matt things she had told no one. Dreams she hadn't had in a long time.

And suddenly, her lungs opened up, like wings on a butterfly, and she could breathe long and vibrant breaths. She told him everything. Her plans for when she returned to Minnesota. How pathetic she felt, having to live back at home and sleep in her childhood bed. How she wanted to travel more, and take charge of her career, her life, and her future.

Matt just listened. He'd give his thoughts once in a while, but he never interrupted the flow of her narrative. When they finally finished their dinner in the North End, she felt alive.

As they walked back toward the hotel through the falling snow he said, "You know, I know some people who would benefit from the same thing you want to do for my uncles. You could probably pick up some business if I spread the word."

"Of course! I would definitely be able to help with logos or branding."

A tiny spark of excitement ignited inside her. She could create designs the way she wanted and create a brand of her own. Kate O'Neil Designs would no longer be just a dream.

"You know what an entrepreneur does when they get their first client?" Matt asked her as they reached the corner. "They celebrate."

"Client?"

"Maybe you could help out a lobster guy?" he said. "I bet even people in Minnesota would want some of Maine's fresh lobster."

She covered her mouth with her hands as she realized what he was saying, then wrapped her arms around his neck, hugging him.

His arms squeezed her, then let go as he said, "This calls for a drink on me," Matt said. "I know just the spot."

"You're my client, which means I should be the one buying the first round."

"Alright, but I get to pick the drink."

There was no mistaking the look he was giving her.

A warm wave from her belly rushed to her chest. "That sounds perfect."

CHAPTER 10

"*H*ere you go." Matt placed a tall glass of a local IPA in front of Katie. "You're going to love this one."

She reached for the foggy glass and took a slow sip. The froth covered her upper lip. She closed her eyes as she swallowed, then set the glass back on the table. "That is good."

Matt took a long drink from his own glass. It was exactly how he wanted to finish his day. There was no other place he wanted to be as the snow pounded down outside.

"Does it always snow this much?" she asked.

Matt looked out the window of the small pub, tucked into a side street in the north end. Thick flakes fell in a steady stream. "Not always, but this system looks like it's going to stick around for a while."

"What a day!" She slapped the table with her hand.

"To Kate O'Neil Designs!" Matt lifted his glass and tapped it against hers.

"To being a world-wide commercial lobsterman." She picked up her glass again and they toasted each other.

She let out a big belly laugh as their glasses touched. "It's funny how a lot of my best days have been with you."

Matt held his tongue. He didn't tell her how she was the best love of his life. Instead, he focused on the Christmas lights sparkling in her eyes.

"Do you remember when we drove through the White Mountains?" The trip down the Kancamagus highway flooded his head.

"You pretended you knew where you were going."

"And I had to drive my mom's minivan."

"Ugh, minivans are the worst." Her expression serious. "I will never own a minivan."

"Aw, they're not that bad." Matt thought of his mom's van, filled with four kids strapped in the back.

"You wouldn't admit we were lost. We passed the same exit three times before you asked someone for directions."

"I wanted to look cool!" Matt defended his teenage self. "If I remember correctly though, it ended up being a pretty cool day."

"A very cool day." Her head tilted, making her hair slide over her shoulders, the light shining off it. "We ended up at that swimming spot."

"Diana's Bath."

"And we drove up that Mountain."

"Mount Washington."

Her eyes crinkled, but glowed at the same time.

"I killed my mom's brakes."

She twirled her drink.

"You know you're going to have to help me haul out those pots," he said. Leaning a bit closer, his hand almost touched hers as it toyed with her coaster.

Her smile became a smirk. She continued to spin her pint glass on the table. "We did dump a few pots out there."

Matt continued playfully, "Unless you're taking off."

She didn't say anything for a moment, and Matt cringed. Why did he have to say that?

"I'm not leaving for a few more days." Katie straightened up in her seat as if she had just decided. "I'll help, but only if you promise to make that lobster dinner with me."

"Deal." Matt immediately smiled. He held out his hand and they shook. The warmth from her skin radiated up his whole body. He held on longer than he should have, but she didn't let go. Their eyes locked.

"Can I get you two anything else?" the server set a bowl of popcorn in front of them.

Katie's hand slipped out from his, and she looked away.

Maybe it was the drink, but he felt as though something had happened between them. Something he couldn't explain, but nevertheless, he felt it.

By the time they left the pub, the streets of Boston were covered in a layer of snow. There were no cars, no people, or any sounds other than their steps crunching as they walked toward the hotel. They stepped into the lobby, and the shiny marble floors squeaked as they walked across them in their snowy boots.

She followed Matt up to the counter as a woman smiled at them. "How can I help you?"

"We're here to check in." Matt brushed off some of the snow on his jacket. "It's under Matt Williams."

"Good evening, Mr. Williams." She gathered a folder, stuffing two key cards into the pockets without even looking. "You will be in rooms 319 and 321, which have an adjoining door."

"Thank you." Matt took the folder.

As they stood by the elevator, dripping snow, Kate closed her eyes as a strong urge to wrap her arms around his neck and kiss him. When she opened her eyes, she saw him staring at her with that smile of his.

There was no doubt his look meant something, but was she ready for something? Was she ready to get her heart broken again? Because the timing couldn't be worse. His divorce, her break-up, and not to mention the seven states in between them.

But he was Matt.

Her Matt.

He was worth a broken heart. She faced him, about to swing her arms around his neck and kiss him, when the elevator doors opened. Another couple stood inside. Matt gestured toward the door, but she could feel the heat coming off him. She took in a deep breath as she stepped inside, gathering herself. Did he feel it, too? As they stood side by side in silence, she swore he could hear the pounding of her heart when his body touched hers.

When the elevator reached the third floor, they soon found themselves standing outside their rooms.

"I had a really nice time tonight," she said.

Matt handed her a key card. "Me, too."

Stalling, she toyed with it, wanting to be the Katie from back in the day, carefree and open-hearted. And just as her inhibitions loosened, they reined her right back in to her rational-Kate self. How would any of this work?

"Well, I should get some sleep." The words rushed out faster than she had meant, which made him stand up straighter.

Her shoulders fell when he backed away toward his door, immediately regretting everything about her behavior. "Matt, I'm–"

"We should probably head back to Camden Cove in the morning, to bring back the van. I'll probably grab breakfast downstairs." He unlocked his door. "You should join me."

The words she wanted to say were on the tip of her tongue. Stop. Don't go. Come back. But she didn't say them. Instead, she said, "Good night."

He smiled. "Good night, Katie."

Matt took a cold shower that night, then stared at the ceiling, wishing he had just taken a chance. Maybe she'd have slapped him, but maybe he wasn't wrong. Maybe he was right about everything. That Katie felt it, too. That they were good together. He should've just gone for it.

Jack would definitely call him a chicken.

He could hardly call it sleep, but by the time he heard movement in Katie's room, he was showered and dressed. He had been watching the sun rise above Boston's harbor, thinking of his own little harbor up north, glad he hadn't made a move. Katie had a whole other life away from Camden Cove. She was a vacation girl, and always would be. Beauty and the lobsterman? Nope, this was a brief interlude in her real life, nothing else.

He stood up, wondering if he should tap on the connecting doors, when he heard a soft knock. He swung the door open and there, on the other side, Katie stood looking absolutely amazing.

"Were you just standing there?" she laughed at his immediacy.

"I was just about to knock, actually."

"Funny." She tilted her head when she was amused he had noticed, which he found adorable.

"You ready to get some breakfast?"

"I was just about to ask you the same thing."

She pointed her thumb behind her into the room. "I'll grab my things and meet you out in the hall."

They headed down to the dining room. The Harbor Hotel had been an extravagance Matt wouldn't have paid for in the past. He didn't need fancy things, like a harbor-facing room in the middle of Boston. But seeing her in the morning, sitting across from her at breakfast, and knowing the whole day was theirs, was the best money he ever spent.

By the time they checked out, the snow had melted on the pavement and the roads were deemed safe by Channel Five news. On the ride back, Katie talked about design ideas she had for his website. They talked logistically about payments, shipments, and his ability to do it all himself. She must've stayed up all night thinking of questions to consider. Who would he market his lobsters to? How would he do the shipping? How would he advertise? All of it spun around him as he tried not to focus on the smell of lavender so close to him.

By the time they reached Camden Cove, they had quieted. He had been using the silence to think things through, make sure it was right. If it felt right, then why did he have so many doubts?

"Do you think your uncle's going to be upset that we had to stay over with the van?"

"Only because he wasn't there." Matt pulled off the exit, sneaking a peek at Katie. He wished he had timed things better, but it was too late to get on the water and grab the traps, and too early to do much else. "I can bring you home before I drop off the van."

She bit her bottom lip. "Sure."

Her focus went out the window as the silence enveloped them again. He pulled up Riverside Road to Vivi's place. "I had a great time."

"I had a really incredible time," she said, holding the door handle. Her thumb tapped against it, then she said, "I have tickets tonight for the playhouse. I wasn't going to go, because they were for me and Eric, but if that's not too weird, we... could?"

His mouth opened, but he hesitated before answering.

She jumped in, saying, "If it's too weird, I can go myself, it's just that I loved going there as a kid."

Then a memory flashed in his head. "Didn't we go together one time?"

She smiled. "Yeah, we saw–"

"Little Shop of Horrors!" they said in unison.

"I forgot about that." He looked out the windshield, thinking of that night. "We're old."

"Shush!" she said. "Was that a yes?"

He laughed. "Only if I can take you out to dinner first. I know this really nice restaurant."

"You do?" she smiled as his playfulness.

"I happen to live above it."

She paused, looking into his eyes. "Then it's a date."

"I'll pick you up at six."

"I can pick *you* up at six," she said, pointing to the minivan sitting in the driveway.

"Six it is." This was his shot.

CHAPTER 11

*J*ust after six, Kate and Matt sat down in the loft of The Fish Market at a two-person table. Jack had really come through for him. Candles lit the small area, glowing off the walls, and ceiling, and Kate's eyes. Flowers sat in a vase on the table. The meal perfect. Their conversation easy.

"So, you two are going to a play?" Jack asked, after they had dessert.

"Yes, Shrek at the playhouse."

Jack had something smart to say that sat on the tip of his tongue, by the smirk on his face, but he held back, which Matt was grateful for. Instead, he said his goodbyes and said, "Don't forget Mr. Palmer is playing donkey this year."

Except for a few changes inside to accommodate for modern technology, the playhouse had remained the same for all these years. As Matt watched the musical of Shrek, he couldn't stop focusing on the fact that Mr. Palmer, his sister's neighbor, was playing Donkey.

"I can't wait to tell Elizabeth," he said, after the lights came up.

She laughed while she clapped. He had started the countdown of when she was leaving in his head already, but tonight it had got to him as she sat in the dark, her face aglow from the stage lights. He couldn't help but wish they could have had another night in Boston. Looking down at his watch as they stood from their seats, he saw that it was already past ten. Where in Camden Cove did you hang out in the middle of winter?

"Want to go to Finn's Tavern?" he asked.

She stopped clapping and faced him. "Yes."

The winter made Camden Cove appear empty during the daylight hours, but by night, a large crowd filled the tavern. The quaint bar looked exactly like one would expect in Maine. Moose antlers hung from the wall alongside fishing nets and lobster paraphernalia. Everyone wore flannel shirts and most sported winter hats. A glow from the wood stove in the corner reflected off the dark lacquered wood.

"This is nice." She took a sip of the coffee he ordered for her.

"Finn's been in business as long as I can remember."

She looked around at the warm setting. Men and women huddled around small tables, while laughter and Bruce Springsteen could be heard over the dull hum of talking. "Why is everyone staring at us?" she asked, looking around the room.

"They're trying to figure out who you are." It would take a day's time in a town like Camden Cove. It didn't help his family usually were the ones who spread it. This time, however, he didn't care. All he cared about was sitting across from Katie.

"How about we pick some songs?" He pulled out his wallet. The juke box hadn't been updated since the late eighties.

From the other side of the tavern, the bell over the door chimed, and he glanced up to see Justine and Freddy walk in. Freddy smiled the second he and Matt made eye contact. He wrapped his arm around Justine's shoulder as he guided her to the bar.

Katie turned in their direction. "I take it you don't care for him."

"Is it that obvious?" Matt tried to cover his disdain.

She shrugged. "You've greeted everyone else in the whole

town." She looked back over her shoulder. He tried to keep his focus on only her, but he quickly glanced their way. Justine's eyes were fixed on him.

"He's not my favorite person." Matt took a long drink from his IPA before adding, "And that's my ex-wife Justine with him."

"Oh…" Her eyes left his and slanted down. She blew on her coffee, but Matt could feel the mood changing. It had made her instantly uncomfortable.

"If it makes any difference, I've always thought Freddy was a donkey." Matt quirked the side of his mouth, showing he was playing.

"Do you want to leave?" She leaned on her elbows. "I completely understand."

Matt shook his head. "Are you kidding? We haven't picked our music."

She smiled, but she wore a look of worry.

"Seriously, I haven't worried about that in a long time, and neither should you." Matt wanted nothing more than to convince her that Justine was in the past and that was where he wanted her to stay, but the awkwardness continued to grow between them.

Then, breaking the silence, Matt's phone began to dance across the tabletop. A selfie of his sister Elizabeth flashed across the screen, but he ignored it. He wanted to reach over the table and grab her hand. Tell her how he couldn't stop thinking of the smell of lavender, and how he lost his train of thought whenever she came near him. His tongue tied up, and no matter how hard he tried to push the words out, they wouldn't come.

He rubbed his sweaty palms on his thighs, accidentally brushing his leg against hers, almost sending him over the table to kiss her. Then, Gretchen broke the silence by coming up from behind with two beers in her hands. "Freddy wishes you a Merry Christmas."

She looked over her shoulder to Freddy. When she turned back to Matt, she said, "He *is* a donkey."

Matt broke out into a laugh so loud that almost everyone, including Justine and Freddy, turned to look at them.

"And Happy New Year!" he shouted to them. He picked up his glass and raised it into the air. Freddy watched from the bar as Justine pretended to look at her phone, but Matt could see her slyly checking them out.

From that point on, it simply didn't matter what happened on the other side of the Tavern. The only thing that mattered at that moment was Katie sitting in front of him.

~

Kate leaned back in her chair and liked the way she felt. A warm buzz from the beer and the heat from the wood stove pulsated throughout her body as she watched the burning embers. The amber glow flickered across Matt's face.

As much as she tried not to, Kate couldn't help sneaking glances at Matt's ex-wife, and Justine did a poor job of pretending to not pay attention to Matt. The guy she was with talked loudly to another couple next to them. Instantly, comparisons filtered through her head. There was no denying Justine's beauty. She had a classic, coastal-casual style that people in the city tried to emulate.

Kate imagined they must've been a handsome couple. She wondered if it was only the fishing that tore them apart. With the way Justine played with a large diamond ring on her finger, she assumed there had to be much more to their story.

Justine continued to twist and center the diamond. She could tell it was big, even from a distance. Kate thought of her own ring, sitting in a box in her suitcase. She wondered what kind of ring Matt would buy.

Then he laughed from across the table.

"What's so funny?" she asked, raising her eyebrow suspiciously.

"I still cannot believe I'm sitting here with you." He shook his head. "I honestly thought I'd never see you again."

"I never expected to see you, either."

Matt leaned forward, a mischievous smile on his face. "How about a walk home in the snow?"

She looked at the clock. It was after midnight, and the snow floated around outside. She jumped off her stool and pulled her coat off the back of her chair. "That sounds like the best idea I've heard all night."

Kate noticed Justine give a sideward glance as she and Matt left Finn's. When they stepped out of the tavern, a silent hush filled the night air. They were the only two people out on the road. She glanced toward the harbor square, just barely making out the lights of the footbridge through the snow.

Matt walked off the edge of the sidewalk and onto the street. Only a few cars were parked along the side, and she followed in his footsteps. They didn't speak, just walked silently in the snow. Then he reached out for her gloved hand and clasped it in his. A tingle ran up her arm as she sucked in a breath.

They continued walking, silently holding hands, until they reached the village square. Matt slowed down and came to a stop in front of the Christmas tree. He didn't let go of her hand as they stood there. The colors of the lights illuminated their faces and gleamed in the freshly fallen snow. "I don't want the night to end. Come up and have a drink."

Every ounce of her being urged for her to say yes, but she hesitated. Was going to Matt's place the right thing to do? She couldn't promise that she'd be able to control herself around Matt. A drink encouraged rash, impulsive decisions that were not her style, but she didn't want to be the same old Kate.

She wanted to be Katie.

She tilted her head up to the sky. This was the kind of moment when she wanted to take everything in. The thick flakes swirled around them as if they stood inside a snow globe. The bottom boughs of the Christmas tree drooped low, touching the ground with pillows of snow. Off in the distance, the ocean waves crashed with their steady beat. Her heart pulsed rapidly as Matt watched her, waiting for her to answer.

She stepped closer to him, the salty air mixed in with his musky scent. He squeezed her hand, and that's when she wrapped her arms around his neck and kissed him. Her inhibitions were gone, and she had never felt so alive in her whole life. Every cell in her body was on fire. Kissing Matt Williams in the middle of Camden Cove in the snow was absolutely exhilarating.

She pressed her lips harder against his as his hands wrapped around her waist and pulled her in closer to him. And suddenly, the spinning and twirling caught her off guard, and she stepped back.

CHAPTER 12

"I'm so sorry," Katie said, her arms sliding from around his neck as she stepped away. Their breath billowed out between them. Matt took her hands and gave them two quick squeezes. Would she remember what that meant? She squeezed back, but took another step away.

"Don't be sorry." He blew out a breath of his own, hardly able to gather his thoughts. "That was amazing."

She bit her lower lip. "I should go."

She may have stopped kissing him, but there was no denying it. She was feeling the same way he did. Matt didn't want whatever this was to end, but he also didn't want to push her. "Let me at least walk you back."

She tightened her grip on his hand and said, "I'd like that."

It took less time then he would've liked to walk back to Vivi's. He kept her hand in his all the way. The soft pitter-patter of snowflakes fell around them. He wanted to tell her everything he was thinking. How the minute he saw her in that minivan on the side of the road, all the old feelings came rushing back. How beautiful she looked in the snow, and on his boat, and standing under the Christmas lights. How he never forgot the last night they were together under the stars when they were kids.

As Katie walked up the driveway, she turned to him. "I had a great time."

"Me, too. Do you still want to haul those pots tomorrow?"

"Yes. When?"

"Nine?" He walked her up to the front stoop. She nodded and squeezed his hand twice before letting go. She remembered.

"Tonight was really amazing," she said.

It took all of Matt's will not to grab her and pull her into him again. Instead, he leaned over and kissed her lightly on her lips. "It's always amazing with you."

Her rosy cheeks deepened a shade. "Until tomorrow."

"Until tomorrow."

Kate leaned against the front door, listening to Matt's footsteps crunch in the snow as he left. Her heart pounded inside her chest.

"Wow." She grinned.

One. Two. Three. Four. She counted his footsteps as they faded away. She stayed propped against the door, her knees a bit wobbly. Her fingertips traced her tingling lips.

What was she doing, kissing Matt? She had committed her life to Eric less than a week ago, and now she was making out like a teenager in the middle of the street. The whole thing was absolutely crazy, especially since she liked it so much, wanted him so badly, and knew if she had stepped foot in his apartment, she wouldn't have stopped again.

"If it gets your mind off of Eric, why not?" her sister Jen said later, over the phone.

"The last thing I need right now is more complication in my life." She said it mostly to herself. "Eric just left me. And Matt just went through a divorce. Not to mention all the distance between us."

"Did you like kissing him?"

"Yeah…" She touched her lips again.

"Then as long as you're okay, who cares?" Jen paused. "You *are* okay

right?"

If her sister had asked her that a couple of days ago, or even yesterday for that matter, she might have said "no". But today, right now, she was better than okay. She was the happiest she'd ever been. "I don't know what it is about this place. Maybe it's all the good memories, but it's exactly where I want to be."

"Then go over there with a bottle of wine. Maybe the best way of getting over Eric," Jen said," "is by getting under Matt."

"Jen!" she scolded, but she looked out over the harbor toward his apartment.

"Or at least, to kiss him again."

She thought back to her first kiss with Matt. It was the Fourth of July, and he had promised to take her out to see the fireworks. That night, he took her to his parents' place and brought her up into the hay loft. They dangled their feet off the edge and looked out. With the barn doors opened wide, they had a perfect view of the harbor off in the distance.

As they sat, he teased her about her accent, and she teased him about his. Once the fireworks began, she could see the whole village light up in blues and reds and whites, the colors reflecting off the water. She didn't notice him looking at her until his fingertips gently turned her chin toward him. The fireworks sparkled in his eyes. He didn't kiss her at first, and she remembered being nervous he wasn't going to, but then he leaned in. She slowly lowered her eyelids as he kissed her softly on the lips. It was just long enough to make her whole body go numb, but ended so quickly that she wished he'd kiss her again as soon as their lips parted.

Her fingertips traced her lips. She still wanted his kiss.

Even through the thick snow, she could see the light on above The Fish Market. If she was going to live *au pif*, now was the time.

~

Matt sank into his couch and watched the snow fall outside. Once again, he was completely confused about what to do when it came to women. One minute Katie was kissing him, and then she stopped cold, like the snow falling around them. And what should he have done? Pulled her back in and kissed her some more, to make up for lost time? Her kiss was voracious. Matt knew she craved more, but something had made her stop.

The guy back home, probably.

The guy who left her. The guy who let her fly across the country by herself. The guy who didn't call to make sure she was alright. The guy who didn't care if she spent the holidays alone. The guy who didn't deserve her.

Matt stood. He wasn't going to let another donkey take something wonderful away from him. He grabbed his coat and opened the door just as Justine's knuckles were about to touch the wood. It took him a second to register her standing there.

"Hi, Matt." She was alone, her purse clutched in her hands. "Can I come in?"

"Now isn't the best time." He zipped up his coat, ready to step outside and close the door behind him.

"It's really important that we talk."

Matt looked across the harbor toward Vivi's house and saw the lights were all out. He was too late. He blew out a deep breath, but didn't say anything, just backed himself inside and opened the door for her to come in. He unzipped his coat and threw it on a chair.

Justine circled the room, the heels of her boots clicking against the wooden floors. "This place looks the same."

He held in a snide remark about her being dressed, but stopped himself. He walked toward the fridge. "Want something to drink?"

"Sure, that'd be great." Justine rubbed her hands together. She was nervous, he could tell. He grabbed two beers. "So… who's the girl?"

Matt rolled his eyes as he opened the fridge. "A friend from out of town."

"She's very pretty."

Matt twisted off the cap and took a sip of his before handing her one. "To what do I owe the pleasure, Justine?"

"It's about the lines being cut out near Perkins Island."

Matt paused before taking another drink. He wasn't expecting her to say that. "What about the lines being cut?"

Justine sat on the couch and placed her purse on the coffee table. "I heard that someone's cutting lines."

"Yeah, so?"

Justine played with the strap of her purse. "I overheard Freddy talking with one of his friends about your territory."

Matt thought back to what his brother told him about Freddy's buddy O'Malley being back in town. "What does this have to do with lines being cut?"

"Freddy gave them money to cut yours."

Matt sat down and put his beer on the coffee table. It felt like the wind had been knocked out of him.

"Are you kidding me?" Matt looked at his ex-wife and thought about all the misery she had caused him, and now this. Now, Freddy was trying to ruin his business, too? "Why are you telling me? Why not go to the police with your suspicions?"

Justine shook her head. "I shouldn't even be here."

"No, you shouldn't." He didn't say anything at first, his teeth grinding. He clenched his hands into fists by his sides. "If something happens, Justine, and Freddy's involved in this…"

He didn't finish the threat.

Justine moved closer to him, grabbing his hand. Tears formed along the edges of her lids. "I haven't stopped loving you, you know."

Matt looked down at the new engagement ring, the diamond

covered her finger. Not like the half carat Matt could afford. "You need to go."

She wiped away a tear before it fell. She pressed herself against him in an embrace, but he didn't return the gesture. He stayed still and didn't look at her.

"I made mistakes, I can recognize that," she said, pushing her hand away. "But you made mistakes, too. I know you still love me, deep down."

He didn't move. He said nothing, just looked out the window, over the walking bridge toward Katie's aunt's house, where all the windows were dark.

Somehow, Kate survived climbing over the bridge. In the harbor below, bells on the boats rang out as they rolled back and forth in the waves. By the time she reached Matt's apartment the snow was so thick, she could barely see in front of her. As she reached his door, she wiped off the ice and her eyes caught him inside. But he wasn't alone. He stood embracing a woman.

Justine.

A strange mix of emotions swept over her as she stood there in the snow with a bottle of wine in her hands. She watched for a second, frozen, then rushed toward the steps. She needed to get out of there as fast as she possibly could.

She clunked down the wooden staircase in her winter boots, tears falling down her face. How could she be so stupid? She didn't know Matt Williams any more than the next guy. He could've been using her, showing her off in front of his ex-wife at the tavern to get her jealous. Well, it must've worked.

The snow fell harder than before, shooting down, pecking at her face. She trudged over the snowbank, stepping onto the street, and heard the familiar scraping of metal rubbing against pavement. The oversized plow pushed the snow until it was at the corner of the road and created a pile so high it blocked the entrance to the footbridge, making it impossible to climb over safely. She was going to have to walk back the long way through town.

She waited in the square as the plow made its way down the street. The same square where only hours ago she was kissing Matt. The Christmas tree was still lit up. She walked past La Patisserie and threw the bottle of wine in the trash bin by the public parking lot. The wind picked up and blew against her as she passed the town library. By the time she made it to the Congregational Church, the snow had become hard pellets bouncing off her face, and she couldn't feel her toes. When she finally made her way to Vivi's cape, her rented minivan could no longer be seen under a frozen pile of snow.

She slammed the front door and had an urge to call Jen back and scream at her for suggesting such a foolish thing to do. A risk she would never have taken without some sort of push. The French could have their *au pif*.

CHAPTER 13

*K*ate woke on the couch with Vivi's cordless phone next to her ear. Before she fell asleep, she had tried calling all the airlines to get a flight out, but once again the snow prevented any available seats.

Everything was gray around her. Even from the couch, she could feel the blustery day. The rawness outside penetrated its way in as the freshly fallen snow whipped around, biting at the window. The shrilling wind drowned out the waves she longed to hear.

Then the image of Matt holding his ex-wife flashed through her head.

She immediately sat up and reached for the remote. She noticed a chill in the air as she tried turning on the television to check the weather, but it didn't turn on. As she stood up, she wrapped the quilt around her shoulders and stuck her hand under the lampshade, twisting the switch. Nothing. She walked into to the kitchen. All the clocks were blank. The power must have gone out while she was sleeping.

She looked out the kitchen window at the driveway. The minivan was covered in snow. The road didn't even seem to have been plowed yet. Even if she wanted to get a flight, she was completely snowed in.

She couldn't believe this was her life.

She walked back to the living room. Her journal sat on the coffee table. All her new lists and plans. All her righteousness. *I am woman, I don't need a man*, notes. Her fake monologue of believing in herself and making her own happiness saturated those pages.

One by one, she ripped the pages from the binding, crumpling them up and throwing them into the fireplace. All her hopes and plans for the future crushed into tiny balls.

Was it so bad that she wanted to have it all? The career, and the guy, and the happily-ever-after? She opened the side table drawer where Vivi left the matches and lit the red matchstick. She stuck the match underneath the papers. Sulfur stung her nose as she watched her dreams go up in flames.

As soon as the flames took hold, so did Kate's regret. She grabbed the burning paper from the flames and pulled out what she could before it caught. She blew out the embers that hung on, burning her hand and dropping the papers onto the wood floor. The flames quickly died, and she tried flattening the crumpled paper, tears streaming down her face as she willed them back to life, but only a few pages were salvageable. The rest were bits and pieces of blackened paper and ash.

Was this how she was going to live from now on? Wanting to burn the past, but too chicken to face the future?

As the wind howled, Kate could just make out the sound of the waves, but she had no use for their soothing repetition today. She looked down at the empty journal. Torn fringes edged the binding and she stared at the blank pages before her.

Kate took the burnt rubble and the pieces of ash and threw it all in the fireplace. She was no longer going to sit and wallow. She would not fall apart. She was not broken because she didn't have a man, because she didn't need one. Cinderella wasn't real, and neither was true love.

And she was going to live *au pif*, but by her darn self.

Matt waited around the bakery until nine-thirty before he decided to head over to find Katie. He wouldn't risk going out on the water with the storm still lingering. Hauling pots wasn't a risk he was willing to take, especially with Katie.

He kept calling Vivi's house, but the number wasn't working. Like his parents, she must've lost power in the night. The longer he waited, the more concerned he became.

"Frank," he said, pulling his collar up before stepping outside, "I'm headed over to Katie's. Will you tell her to wait here if I miss her?"

"Sure thing." Frank said.

Even with four-wheel drive, the roads were a mess. He should've just gone to the house first and checked on her. He knocked on the front door, bouncing on the balls of his feet as he stood in the cold. The snow had tapered off, but the plow hadn't come yet, and from the looks of the streets around town, it would be awhile.

He waited, then hit the doorbell, but he didn't hear anyone inside. He checked his watch, trying to figure out what to do. With his hands covering his eyes, he peeked through the side window, but didn't see anyone. Where was she?

He'd leave a note. He made his way toward his truck and pulled out his phone. He'd text his friend Dan to be sure to swing by Vivi's with the plow.

Just as he opened his truck's door, he heard the garage door being manually opened. As it lifted up, Katie's feet emerged, and then he saw the rest of her. Once again, his breath was swept away. She didn't see him at first, grabbing a shovel and stepping out into the driveway.

When she did see him, she stopped, but then averted her eyes as she headed to the heap of snow on her car.

Matt shut his truck's door and walked toward her. Glad to see she was home and alright. "Good morning."

Katie didn't say anything. Instead, she walked past him and shoveled the snow behind the minivan. Something was off. He could feel it right away. Was she ignoring him?

"I have a plow coming to take care of the driveway, but it's going to be a while before someone comes," he said. He patted his jacket pockets for gloves, but he'd left them in his truck. "Got another shovel?" He wished he'd thrown one in the back of his truck before leaving. "I can help."

She didn't respond, but appeared to put more effort into digging out the snow. Then as quickly as she started, she staked the shovel into the ground before stomping back toward the house. She came back with a broom and dusted off the snow piled on the roof. What was going on with her?

When finally she looked at him, her eyes were narrow, almost suspicious.

He decided he'd rather be shoveling than standing there and looking like a fool. He grabbed the shovel and started to dig when she stomped over and said, "Stop. I don't need your help."

Matt straightened up and leaned his weight on the shovel's handle. He was equally amused and confused by what was happening. "Well, it appears you're bent on getting your car out."

"I don't need anyone to help me." She brushed the broom's bristles against the back window, spraying Matt with the fresh powder.

The snow melted against his face as he wiped it off. "Are you okay?"

"I'm fine." She stomped toward him again and swiped the shovel from his hand. "Perfect. Now if you don't mind, I have things to do."

Having lived with enough women in his life, he knew what *fine* meant. Matt couldn't wrap his head around what was wrong. Did he do something, or say something to upset her? Because she was anything but fine. When he left last night, things seemed good, really good. Now it was as if she couldn't stand the sight of him.

"Are you upset with me?" Wasn't she the one who blew him off this morning? "I came to tell you we shouldn't go out on the boat."

She huffed. "Figures, you'd cancel."

"It's not really the perfect day for a boat ride." Matt held up his bare hands, making an obvious gesture at the snow.

She twisted her face before she said, "Why don't you take Justine instead?"

"What?" Matt was taken aback, shocked by her use of his ex-wife's name. Either he was in the twilight zone, or she had gone completely mad.

She returned her attention back to cleaning off the van, getting nowhere fast.

"What's going on, Katie?" Matt knew two things. Something had happened between last night and that morning, and he was the object of her contempt. "What's making you so upset?"

Fire burned in her eyes as she threw the shovel down, sinking it into the snow. "Did you plan on taking me home before or after you saw her at the Tavern?"

He thought back to the night before. He had tried so hard to behave nonchalantly in front of Justine and Freddy. As though being around his ex-wife and the man she slept with for months during their marriage was no big deal. He guessed he was more transparent than he thought. But how did being uncomfortable around his ex-wife have anything to do with her being upset?

"I'm sorry if you were uncomfortable." He stepped closer, but she instantly backed away.

"I saw you." She seethed the words through her teeth. "I saw you two together."

Matt ran the night through his head. They had dinner, went to the play, grabbed a drink at the tavern, he walked her home, and then they kissed. Which he thought was great, really great. "Wait... did you come to my place last night?"

"When you two were together." Katie grabbed the shovel and began to dig around the buried vehicle.

He shook his head. "We were just talking."

"Must've been quite the conversation." She picked up the shovel.

"Let me just explain," he said. He replayed the scene with Justine. Her hug. "It's not what you think."

"I think you should leave."

"If you had stayed one second longer, you would've seen that—"

"I would've seen what I should've seen from the beginning." She stabbed the shovel into the snow.

"I promise you it's not what you think." He couldn't believe Justine had messed things up again.

"You're just like all the other guys."

Matt felt her insult, and became equally annoyed. He wasn't like the others. Not to Justine, not to his family, and certainly not to her. "You were the one who stopped whatever was happening last night, remember?"

"I would've never started had I known you had other intentions."

"What intentions are you talking about? I didn't ask Justine to stop by." Matt held his hands in the air. "You know what? I don't need to explain myself to you."

"That's so typical," she hissed at him as he walked away. "You don't owe anything to anyone. You only think of yourself."

He turned to face her. "Who are you talking about?" He waited for her to answer, but she said nothing. "Who are you really mad at?"

As she stood there, he could see tears well up in her eyes. He had crossed a delicate line, even with her being as obnoxious as she was.

"Nothing happened between Justine and me." He stuffed his hands in his pockets as she stood mute. "But this isn't about Justine or me, is it?"

"What's that supposed to mean?" Her eyes narrowed.

"Why didn't you ever call me back all those years ago?" Matt had wanted to ask this question for years.

"What?" She shook her head. "Are you serious right now?"

"Absolutely serious," Matt said. "You just kept me hanging on, waiting for you. You didn't even have the balls to break it off."

"I was a kid."

Matt was disappointed in her answer. "You used me back then, and you used me now, to get over your fiancé."

"I wasn't using you."

"Then why didn't you call me?" Matt held her eyes. "What? Is a fisherman not good enough for you?"

"If you wanted us to work out so badly, then why didn't you come to Minnesota and visit me?"

"You never asked me."

Katie's mouth opened, but she closed it again. She stood in the middle of the driveway, not saying a word, but there was nothing to say. He had been right all along. He waited for her to say something, but when she didn't, he turned toward his truck. Nothing good would come from arguing when she couldn't see the real problem.

She didn't trust him.

As he got inside his truck, his phone began to ring and he looked at the caller ID. Camden Cove Police Department. He answered as he looked out at her still standing in the snow. "Hello?"

"Matt, its Alex." His friend's voice on the other line sounded serious. "I think you should come down to the docks."

CHAPTER 14

*K*ate looked in the mirror. Her black eyes had faded into a light twinge of olive green. She wondered what her heart would look like if it were on the outside. She now knew what shame looked like.

The hurt in Matt's eyes when he walked away said everything. She had used him. And worse, she treated him badly. It was one thing to assume the worst, but to become so ugly to someone who had only been kind to her… always. Even the day Matt stole her heart, he had been nothing but kind to her.

She could still remember how hot it was that day. She came out of the library with a pile of books in her hands. Her refuge from the mundane routine she had fallen into with Vivi that summer. As soon as she stepped into the sun, the heat hit her and sweat dripped down her face. She stopped walking and wiped her forehead with the back of her hand, balancing the books in her arms.

That's when he pulled over.

He rolled down the window and called out, "Your name's Katie, right?"

She slowed, wishing that of all the times to run into him, it hadn't been on the hottest day on record in Maine. She was already drenched after walking out of the air-conditioned library and hardly a block up the street.

"Um, yeah." She didn't want to admit it, hoping she could have a second chance run-in when she had actually showered and didn't have her hair up in a rat's nest on top of her head.

"Do you need a ride?"

Kate looked at him, embarrassed by her glistening exterior. "No, thank you."

He then introduced himself. "I'm Matt, Matt Williams. My grandmother is friends with your aunt. You're the girl from Minnesota, right?

She nodded, surprised that he still remembered her. "You're the sea glass kid."

A smile grew as he nodded. "Are you sure you don't want a ride?"

Her sunglasses slipped as she studied him. The boy she had met those summers ago was no longer little. He was a young man. His green eyes drew her in. And his killer smile left her tongue-tied. His tan arms were defined with muscle she hadn't seen in the sixteen-year-old boys back home.

She absolutely wanted a ride. Then, all of her insecurities piled higher than the stack of books in her hands and she chickened out. "That's okay. I can walk."

She turned before he could say anything else and walked away, but as she did, her bundle of books slipped from her hands and tumbled to the ground. Covers opened like butterflies, pages splayed in the grass.

Matt cut the engine before jumping out of the car, and helped collect the books off the ground.

"I haven't read this one." He held up *My Travels with Charlie*. "You'll have to let me know if you liked it."

"Have you read Steinbeck before?" She picked up the rest of the books from the ground. Books filled with adventures she had only dreamt about.

"For school, but I liked him." Matt shrugged. "Do you?"

She nodded as he continued to stand there. Her throat tightened up, unable to continue a conversation.

"Are you learning to surf?" Matt asked, pointing to one of the books in her hands.

She looked down at the pile and felt as though he could see inside her soul from her choices. She looked back up at him. "I don't have a surfboard, but I saw that you can rent them at the beach."

"I could teach you." Matt blocked the sun's rays with his hand and looked out toward the harbor. "Tomorrow morning will be high tide. We can meet at Perkins beach. Where I took you before."

At first, she didn't answer; just bit her bottom lip to keep from smiling too widely. He remembered her from collecting sea glass. A bead of sweat rolled down her forehead, slipping onto her ear. What did she have to lose?

"That would be incredible."

His smiled as he asked, "Are you sure you don't want a ride?"

For the rest of the summer, they spent every day together. She remembered the urgency to see him, that feeling of wanting to be near him, even if it was only for a second. Just to see him. She thought of nothing else but him. She fell in love with Matt Williams that summer.

Now, as she looked at her reflection in the mirror, she realized she never stopped loving him.

Just then, a buzzing broke out. Everything in the house turned back on, taking over the silence and stirring her out of her thoughts. Without stopping to think, she picked up the phone and dialed the 1-800 number on the back of her ticket.

As soon as someone picked up, she said, "I need a flight out of Portland as soon as possible."

~

Matt stood, speechless, looking at the one corner of Maggie Mae still visible above the waterline. Alex Martinez stood by his side as the Coast Guard investigated his boat.

Matt rubbed his beard with his hand. Justine's words haunted him.

"Do you know anyone who would want to do this?"

Matt shook his head. "Nope. I haven't heard anything."

Matt didn't need to lead him to Freddy Harrington. If Freddy was involved like Justine said, then the connection would be revealed at some point. Plus, Matt wouldn't mind getting to him before Officer Martinez. In the meantime, what was he going to do?

"I'll call some other marinas and see if they've seen anything." Alex pulled out his radio. "If you hear anything, you need to let me know. Don't follow some old fisherman's code when it's your livelihood on the line."

Matt nodded as he looked at Maggie Mae. Things couldn't get much worse than this. Everything he had worked for had literally sunk into the harbor's waters. It would cost tens of thousands of dollars to fix her. He hoped insurance would cover it.

His eyes traced the harbor's shore to Katie's cottage. Even with everything happening around him, he couldn't stop thinking about the way he'd talked to her. It wasn't fair to bring up the past. The fact was, he didn't even care about his boat at this point. She was all he cared about, and now he had lost her again.

CHAPTER 15

ate's flight was in less than three hours. She needed to pack, clean up, and throw her luggage in the van.

As soon as she stepped outside, the view of the harbor made her stop. The sight of Camden Cove, even as her life spun out of control, still stole her attention. She noticed Matt's boat missing from the harbor, as other lobster boats bobbed in the water as the tide crept in. Seagulls swept through the sky in the wind. The chiming of the church bells off in the distance reminded her of the time, and the beauty shattered as the reality of heading back home hit her.

As soon as the van was cleaned off, she threw her luggage in the back. But the familiar grinding of steel against the pavement, crunching in the background made her freeze.

The plow was coming.

"You've got to be kidding me." She slammed down the lift gate and rushed to the driver's seat. Once inside, she swiveled the rearview mirror to see what she already knew. The orange over-sized truck barreled down Riverside Road. The bane of her existence since coming to this sleepy town would plow her in if she didn't move it.

She threw the minivan in reverse and slammed her foot against the gas. The plow continued on its path, roaring down the street, thrusting the snow onto the sidewalk and into driveways. She took her chances and gunned it. The tires slipped in the cold mess, sending the van toward the embankment on the other side of the driveway. With only a few yards to go, she straightened the wheel and returned her foot on the gas. She needed to make it out.

Then she heard the roar of the plow's horn, warning her of its presence. It only made her press the gas with more vigor. The van's wheels jumped the embankment and pulled back into the driveway. The plow continued to move forward, metal screeching as the truck began to brake. She only had a few feet before the three-ton blade of steel would be on top of her. And then, just when she had a glimmer of hope, the minivan slid back into the side of the driveway, slamming deeper into the snowbank. The high-pitched screech of her tires spinning masked the sound of the plow's horn.

The plow roared to a stop, pushing snow against its blade in the middle of the driveway, burying the rear end of the van that she'd spent an hour shoveling out.

"What the heck do you think you're doing?!" the driver yelled out his window. "Are you trying to get killed? Snowplows have the right of way!"

Kate jumped out of the van and yelled back, "Don't you people have any decency? You saw that I was coming! Can't you do your job without torturing those around you?"

The man continued shouting as he rolled up his window, putting the truck into reverse.

She screamed into the sky, "Why must the universe punish me?!"

She kicked the snow around her and then pounded the side of the minivan as the plow drove away. She threw her head back and growled a scream. She yelled into the gray sky, but the sea held more rage. Its waves crashed into the granite cliffs, muting her wrath, and it just made her even more mad.

The tears came even though she fought to keep them at bay. She did not want to cry. She did not want to be defeated, to be pathetic. She didn't want to be a victim. She no longer wanted to be that Kate.

The noose wrapped around her chest.

What now?

Kate fell backwards and sunk into the snow. It enveloped her and muted everything around her. All she could hear was her breath—it was short and quick, and low on oxygen. She laid there and tried to focus. One. Two. Three. Breathe.

She counted again, but it didn't help. The noose was too tight.

She thought about going back, seeing Eric, having to tell everyone about the engagement, going back to work and then moving her stuff out and into her mom's place. She still hadn't even told her mom.

Did she calculate her self-worth by being attached to a man?

And suddenly Kate realized her biggest problem was *her*.

How badly did she need the fairytale to be happy?

She sat up on her elbows from the cold cocoon as the snow-plow grated down another road. She wiped away the snow from her face. She wasn't going to apologize for wanting it all, but she certainly wasn't going to wait for a knight in shining armor to come around. She needed to figure out what would make her happy on her own.

She brushed off as she stood, and went directly inside. She grabbed her torn-up journal. If she was ever going to find happiness, she would have to face her demons. With the last of the blank pages, she began to write. The words poured out of her. She wrote about things she'd never allowed herself to say out loud, or even admit. She wrote about her fears, her assumptions, and her doubts about herself.

She wrote about Eric.

She wrote about her parents' divorce.

She wrote about what she wanted in life.

Then she wrote about Matt.

When the words stopped pouring out, she looked out at the horizon as the clouds opened up and a ray of sun, like a torch from the heavens, lit the water below.

And then different words came itching out of her pen and her story suddenly changed.

The noose loosened. She took a deep breath.

Thoughts spun around her head and her blood began pumping through her veins. Things she had only dreamed about starting to be planned out on paper. Exciting dreams she never felt worthy of, nor dared to plan out.

Then, the house phone began to ring, jolting her out of her thoughts.

She rushed to the kitchen. "Hello?"

"Katie." There was only one other person who called her by that name. Vivi. "Katie, I'm coming home early to see you before you leave."

Tears welled up in her eyes, not because of sadness or shame or pain, but from joy. True joy. "I can't wait."

Matt watched as he had Maggie Mae towed toward the marina in Portland. There, she'd get fixed up as good as new. The only question he had was, how long would it take before he could go back out on the water? Maybe with it being the off season, they'd be able to get right to work on it, but Matt figured it'd be the opposite.

As he watched Maggie Mae head north and disappear from view, he didn't think things could get much worse for him. His boat had sunk in the harbor. His ex-wife's fiancé might be on a mission to destroy him. And the Coast Guard wanted to talk to him about his own involvement in the sinking of his ship.

He'd handle the problems with the boat and with Freddy. He

wasn't worried about the Coast Guard, and knew they were following procedure. What he couldn't handle was the possibility of Katie never understanding how he felt about her. Did he go for broke, and go back? Try to make her understand? Should he tell her the truth. That he was in love with her, and didn't want to lose her ever again.

He looked at his empty slip at the dock. Why would Katie stay? Especially after everything with Justine. Sure, nothing happened, but the history and the drama seemed to linger and continue to haunt him. Last night was just a preview of the years to come. Who would want to deal with that? He didn't want to deal with that. All he brought to the relationship was an over-bearing family and deep-seated struggles from past relationships.

"Mr. Williams, we won't take up too much of your time," said the officer of the Coast Guard, "but we'd like you to come down to the office and answer a few questions."

Matt stuffed his hands in his pockets and nodded. "No problem."

He looked over to Katie's cottage. It had been hours since their fight. He wondered if that was the last time he'd see her. He followed the officer back down the dock toward the parking lot.

She was better off without him.

Elizabeth sat in her favorite spot at the bakery and watched Camden Cove from the window. She cupped her hands around the fancy hot cocoa Frank had given her, but it was David's almond biscotti she dipped in the cocoa that she really came for.

Through the window she noticed Kate, walking down the street with a certain determination that was new. Her chin was up, her hair floating behind her as she pounded down the street. She swung open the door to the bookstore and went inside. Elizabeth hadn't even finished her biscotti before Kate came back out with bags in her hands. She turned on her heel and went inside the Camden Cove Country Store, right next door.

Frank came out from behind the counter, his attention on Kate as well.

"She looks like she's on a mission," he said, standing next to her and looking out the window.

"Mom told me Matt has been taking her out on the town." Elizabeth smiled, thinking of the two together. It'd be nice for her brother to have something good again. Even as teens Elizabeth had the two matched, but the timing wasn't in their favor.

"It's such a shame she lives so far away," Frank said, looking out at her.

Elizabeth nodded in agreement. "Yes, she's lovely."

She wondered how involved Frank had been in this newly blossoming relationship, as they watched her come out of the Country Store with more bags in her hands. Then, without stopping, Kate headed down the road and into the flower shop. The whole spectacle made them delightfully curious.

Customers entered the bakery, and Frank went behind the counter. Elizabeth continued to keep an eye out the window, waiting for Kate to emerge onto the street. Finally, she came out from the flower shop's door with a couple of bouquets tucked in the crook of her arms. She stepped out from under the green awning and looked up, closing her eyes, letting the sun touch her face.

Kate looked different.

Then, with a little skip, she crossed the street. Scooting her chair over, Elizabeth strained to see Kate jog up the staircase that led to Matt's apartment. She knocked and looked around her. Matt didn't appear to be home. With one more knock, she twisted a bag off her arm and hung it on the door handle, inside the screen.

She skipped down the stairs and then jumped off the last step, and Elizabeth knew what had happened.

Kate had found her joy.

CHAPTER 16

*A*s Kate walked around town, she tried to ignore the fact that Maggie Mae wasn't in her boat slip. The docks could be seen from Harbor Lane. After every store, she peeked over, hoping to catch Matt, to apologize for her behavior, but neither he nor Maggie Mae ever returned.

When she reached the bakery, she made sure it was near closing time, so she could talk to both Frank and David without being a bother. Her heart raced as she entered, the aromas luring her to step further inside. She looked around, and the place was empty except for Frank.

He stopped wiping the table when he noticed her. "Hello, Kate."

His friendly smile made her nerves calm a bit, but she still didn't know what to say at first. Exhaling, she asked, "Do you and David have a free moment?"

Frank eyed her as though she piqued his curiosity. "Sure, let me go grab him."

"You don't have to, right now." She was starting to chicken out. She grabbed the straps of her computer bag. "I can wait."

"No, it's no problem," he said. "He'd love to see you."

Kate paced around in a one-foot radius as Frank went into

the kitchen. She bit her lower lip as she thought of how she was going to broach the fact that she thought they needed to fix their website, without sounding insulting.

"Hello!" David said, as he and Frank walked out from the kitchen. "Do you need something?"

"I don't need anything." Kate pulled out her computer and set it down on the table in front of them. She opened it up, and the sample website she'd created covered the screen. On the heading, La Patisserie was written a bold elegant script in a deep chocolate. It reminded her of a blend of coffee that would go well with one of David's desserts. A close-up of a chocolate canele covered the rest of the page. All the different layers of chocolate had been highlighted by the different textures and shades.

"It's beautiful," Frank said as he sat down in front of the computer. David stood behind him as Frank scrolled the page with the different links she had made.

"It's just a sample, but I'd like to redesign your website as a way to say thank you." She looked at the two of them. The smiles on their faces couldn't be mistaken.

Frank looked back at David, then over to Kate. "This is exactly what we needed."

He continued to scroll through the page as she explained her ideas for each strip.

"The best part of your bakery is you two," she said, as they reached the section titled "Our Story". She knew from a marketing standpoint that people loved feeling part of something.

"I can't believe you have all the links and plug-ins," Frank said. "You even set up a newsletter?"

"You can post recipes and start collecting emails, you can market the summer tourists with your newsletter by letting them know of the different classes you're offering, and special events." She clicked, and a page for David's cooking classes flashed on the screen. "There's even a link to pay, here."

"The layout is fantastic," David said. "How'd you do all this?"

"This is what I do." She shrugged. "I hope I'm not offending you by suggesting you get rid of your old website."

"We made that in haste." David walked over to her and gave her a hug. "My dear, this is one of the most generous gifts we've ever received."

She couldn't hold back her smile. She didn't know why, but his words struck her heart, and tears formed. She quickly wiped a fallen tear and inhaled a deep breath. "This is the least I could do to show my gratitude for your friendship."

"You are not just a friend, you're family now."

When Matt finished with the Coast Guard, he pulled into Vivi's driveway. Katie's van was there, but there was no sign of her. When he knocked on the door, no one answered. Maybe she was avoiding him, although the house did appear empty. He hated that he'd left the way he did. She didn't owe him anything. He was just as much to blame. He'd let her go. Just like he let Justine go. He didn't really hold onto anything, did he? He didn't fight for them, just let them slip through his fingers without grabbing hold.

He looked out toward the harbor at his empty slip. That boat had been everything he thought he ever wanted, but now she was just a boat. She wasn't even a *she*. As he stood alone on Vivi's front step, he wondered if that was it, for him.

His life felt like a Shakespearean drama unfolding. If he wanted things to work out, he'd have to be willing to leave the things he loved behind. He'd have to be willing to leave fishing, his family, and everything for her, because he couldn't ask her to do the same thing for him. He hadn't done that with Justine, and looked where that got him.

He turned toward the afternoon sun now sinking behind the trees, casting shadows of pine silhouettes over the white snow. He had seen this moment almost every day coming in from the water, but never paid attention while on land. He looked out toward the village and saw his family's restaurant, his uncles' bakery, the Congregational church and his neighbor's roofline. He looked at the beach where he learned to surf, and the street where he broke his leg skateboarding. He saw his best friend Dan's house, where he'd spent half his childhood. This was his home.

Could he leave his whole life behind?

He took one last peek through the front window. Even if she were home, if she hadn't answered by now, then she clearly didn't want to talk to him.

When he got in his truck and pulled out, he headed over to his parents' place. He hadn't planned on stopping by, but he wanted to get his mind off things. If he went home, he'd just keep thinking about the day, and probably make things worse by continuing to bother Katie.

When he walked in the door, his sisters sat around the kitchen counter with his mother. They all looked at him as though he was exactly who they were talking about.

"Ladies," he said cautiously.

"I didn't know you were stopping by." Sarah stood and grabbed a mug, filling it with coffee.

He kissed his mother on the cheek as she handed him the mug. "Thanks."

"Dan told us about Maggie Mae," Elizabeth said. Each one of the Williams women's faces showed concern. They *were* talking about him. "What happened?"

"Alex doesn't know." Matt decided to keep Justine's visit to himself, but the more he rolled it over in his mind, the more he felt Freddy was somehow involved. He leaned against the counter. "He noticed it had sunk this morning, but it could've happened sometime last night."

"Do they think it's foul play?"

Matt nodded. "Whoever's doing the vandalism around the

cove has hit three of the lobstermen that happen to fish off Perkins Island."

"All with the same grandfather," his mom said. She had the same suspicions, apparently.

"Well, people will start talking," his father said as he got up from his recliner. "Watch, someone will say something."

"Good thing you have insurance," Sarah said.

"It's the headache more than anything." Matt shook his head.

"Do you think it's Freddy?" John asked, coming out and saying what everyone was skirting around.

Matt shrugged. "The Coast Guard is looking into things, but Alex said he'd check around as well."

John nodded. "I'll make a few phone calls and see if anyone's heard anything in town."

"Lauren and I are going to the tavern in a little bit," Elizabeth said, looking at her phone. "We could listen for any talk."

Matt asked. "Where's Adam?"

"He's at home, watching a movie with Lucy," she said. "And we're having a girl's night with Rachael."

Matt thought of Freddy and his run-in at Finn's with Katie. He'd bet Maggie Mae he'd be there again tonight, especially if he was involved somehow. Freddy would be that cocky, to be a showboat about it. He'd like to have a conversation with him either way. "I think I'll come with you."

"But it's a girl's night." Elizabeth pulled out her phone and began typing, probably texting Adam, like always. Matt could feel his own phone burning in his front pocket. He wanted to call Katie. He wanted to tell her how much of a jerk he was, but he knew he wasn't being fair either way. She deserved better.

"I thought you'd be going out with Katie again," Lauren said with amusement in her voice. Even though it was said in good fun, it annoyed him all the same.

Elizabeth turned to him and suggested, "You should invite her along!"

He shook his head and grabbed his coat. "Nope."

Sarah then looked concerned. "Are you going to see her before she leaves?"

He turned to Elizabeth and asked, "Didn't you mention something about Finn's?"

Lauren rolled her eyes, but he could see his mother and sisters wanted an answer.

"I'd love to catch up with her," Elizabeth said. "Invite her."

"Not tonight." He tried to sound nonchalant about it all, but he could feel the room getting warmer and smaller the longer they looked at him. "She's busy."

"Come on, invite her," Lauren pleaded.

He knew they meant well, and they wouldn't stop if he didn't answer. So he took the casual approach and shrugged. "She's not home, I tried."

"Well, I bet if you just called her—"

"Let's go," Matt cut his mother off.

Elizabeth's eyes met Sarah's, and they both looked to Lauren. Sarah opened her mouth to say something but Lauren, reading the tension in the room, jumped off her stool and said, "We should get going."

Matt nodded and grabbed his coat. He kissed his mother goodbye, but didn't say anything more, afraid he might say something he'd regret. Finn's was a much better choice.

Elizabeth insisted she and Lauren had to drive separately to pick up Rachael, and since Matt wasn't willing to argue with her, he was happy to meet them there. When he walked in, he was immediately submersed into the holiday crowd. Families visiting for Christmas and New Year's filled the tight quarters, standing around tables and taking most of the tables.

Matt went to the bar as Elizabeth, Lauren and Rachael made their way inside, grabbing a table as a group left.

"Girl's night for you, too?" Finn, the bartender, asked. Rachael's grandfather never cut Matt any slack.

"We'll have four of whatever's on tap," he said over the crowd.

Finn dropped a shot glass in front of Matt and filled it with whiskey. "Heard about the boat." He passed the glass over to Matt. "Hope they catch whoever's causing trouble."

Matt nodded a thank you. Finn had owned the tavern for the past thirty years, and most of his customers were regulars, Freddy being one of them. He, if anyone, would probably hear things.

"Have you heard any grumblings?" Matt asked.

Finn shook his head. "I'll keep a listen out for anything."

"Thanks, Finn." He held up the shot glass and threw it back. The burn down his throat was a pleasant feeling compared to the way his chest had hurt all day.

He carried the four beers to the table.

"To Maggie Mae." He lifted up his beer and took half of it down in one fell swoop.

"Are you going to be okay?" Elizabeth asked.

He wrapped his fingers around the glass, sucked the rest down, and smacked it onto the table. "Yup."

Elizabeth leaned closer as if trying to read his expression. "Is this only about your boat?"

"Somebody tried to sink my boat, what else do I need to be upset about?" Matt slid the glass to the middle of the table and grabbed Lauren's beer out of her hands.

"Do we have to spell it out for you?" Elizabeth sounded like Sarah.

"Spell what out?"

"She's perfect for you," Lauren blurted out, rolling her eyes.

"You two should leave it alone." Matt took a long drink of her beer. He was not talking about Katie tonight.

Rachael's eyes perked up. "Are you guys talking about the new woman in town?"

"Yes, Kate." Elizabeth shook her head at him. "You know we're right."

"It would never work." Matt leaned his elbows on the table and rubbed his hands together. He cocked his head toward her. "I can't just pack up and go to Minnesota."

"Why the heck not?" Lauren sighed as though he was the immature twenty-something. "No one said you have to get married."

"Because I messed up this time. That's why."

"What?" the three women said together.

He leaned back in his seat, exhaling loudly. He didn't want to get into it with the three of them, especially his sisters. "Last night, Justine stopped by, and apparently she saw us together."

"You and Justine?" Elizabeth said it loud enough for others around them to hear. Her face turned redder by the second. "If you and Justine get involved again, I promise I will—"

"Will you be quiet?" Matt looked around the tavern. "I don't need the whole town knowing my business."

"If you and Justine start up again, I promise I will lose it," she whispered through her teeth.

"Nothing happened," he said, "but Katie wouldn't listen."

"Then go tell her again."

"You don't get it." He squeezed his glass. "She's not going to go for a fisherman. A girl like Katie doesn't settle for a guy who lives out in the sticks and smells like chum all day long."

"I think you're wrong."

"Well, you don't have to think about it, because I know she wants nothing to do with me."

Before she could say anything else, the bell on the door opened and stole their attention. Freddy Harrington and his buddies walked into the bar. Freddy's smug face brightened as he noticed Matt sitting on the other side of the room.

"You've got to be kidding me," he said, as Freddy cut across the room to their table.

"You're going to have to try a little bit harder than that, Williams," Freddy's voice carried throughout the small space and grabbed everyone's attention. "Justine wants nothing to do with you."

"I don't know what you're talking about." Matt jumped off his stool. "But I'd like to know how my boat ended up at the bottom of the harbor this morning."

"I don't know what you're talking about." Freddy repeated Matt's words through his smirk.

Matt looked at Freddy's slim build, his slender physique would be pummeled by his years of pulling up pots from the heavy ocean water. It wouldn't be a fair fight. But he wanted nothing more than to punch him in the face right then.

Freddy turned to the bar and yelled, "A round of drinks on me to celebrate my recent engagement!"

People around the room cheered and thanked him, but it was obvious they knew what Freddy was doing. Conversations had all but stopped as everyone watched what was unfolding between them.

Matt looked down and noticed Freddy's fist had tightened up.

Freddy's upper lip curled when he said, "A wedding can bring such joy."

Matt laughed, and Freddy charged him. Lauren leaped in front of them.

"Let's grow up, gentlemen," Lauren said, pushing Matt back toward his seat.

"I hear Williams aren't really the marrying kind," Freddy said, loud enough for others to hear. "Kyle has told me stories!"

It all happened in slow motion. Lauren's face dropped, Elizabeth gave Matt a nod, and he didn't hesitate to swing his right fist, nailing Freddy right where their father had taught them to hit. The knuckle shot, he called it. Freddy stumbled back, grabbing the side of his face.

"What the!" Freddy said, holding his jaw. "You'd better get yourself a lawyer this time."

"Walk away, Williams!" One of Freddy's cronies pushed Matt back.

Most of the crowd watched wide-eyed, but when Freddy gained his balance, he brushed his hands through his hair. "No wonder Justine feels sorry for you and your pathetic family!"

Finn spoke toward Freddy. "You boys need to take this some-place else."

"No need. It's settled." Matt pulled out his wallet and threw money down on the table. He had had enough for the night. "Drinks are on me."

As Matt walked past Freddy, he grabbed his shirt. "Never speak about my family again."

Elizabeth smiled as he dropped Freddy from his clutches. He walked straight through the crowd and out the door. As he headed down the sidewalk toward his apartment, Elizabeth came out of the tavern.

"Wait up!" she yelled out.

He stopped but didn't look at her, his whole body shaking with adrenaline and anger. What kind of game was Justine playing by telling Freddy about going to his apartment?

"Well, I guess he heard a different version of what happened last night," Elizabeth said as she pulled out her keys. "Need a ride?"

"I can walk." His teeth ground together as he thought about the games his ex-wife always played.

"Do you think Freddy sunk your boat because of last night?" Elizabeth looked at him, concerned.

"Probably." Matt moved his fingers to check if anything was broken.

"His brother told him stories?" Lauren slammed open the tavern's door with Rachael right behind her. Her fingers were blazing across her screen. Her phone started ringing. She walked down the sidewalk a bit before she answered. "You'd better tell me what your brother means by all the stories *you've* told him about me."

Elizabeth zipped up her coat. "Look, you may have lost a boat, but it can be replaced. Kate, however, is not sticking around forever."

He didn't respond, he needed to walk away. His sister was wrong. It was already too late. Katie wanted nothing to do with him. And with the way the night ended, he knew there'd be more run-ins with Freddy and Justine. This would be dragged out, just like their relationship. He didn't want Katie to have to be a part of it. All his problems were like fishing. They'd all be here for another season, another year, everything exactly the same.

As he climbed the steps to his apartment, his eyes wandered over to the harbor to Katie's. The house was completely lit up. He stopped half-way up and just stared at it. Wondering what she was doing inside. Wishing he could go back in time and do it all over again.

He grabbed the railing and felt the throbbing of his knuckles, returning his thoughts to reality. That's when he noticed a bag with a bow hanging on his doorknob. He ran up the steps, took it off the handle and opened it. He pulled out a book from inside. *My Travels with Charlie,* by John Steinbeck.

"Katie."

~

Christmas music blasted as Kate made the final touches around the house. The Charlie Brown tree she'd rescued from the garbage was back up and decorated. Lights twinkled and reflected in the windows. She found the ornaments in the attic storage, and placed them carefully on the tree. Vivi had kept everything, homemade decorations from all the generations. A warm feeling washed over her, like she was home.

She couldn't wait to see Vivi tomorrow.

She poured herself a cup of coffee as she finished uploading the last of her photos on La Patisserie's new website. David and Frank's response was exactly what she hoped for. It gave her the motivation to push forward and plan out her own website for Kate O'Neil Designs.

Tomorrow she would buy a new phone and start figuring out her first strategy for networking and marketing her business. Her own business.

She looked out the kitchen window as she made pastries from the ingredients David had given her. The harbor twinkled in the night. Once again, she looked at the red bag hanging on Matt's door. Her anxiety was no less than before. He hadn't been home since she dropped it off. The boat slip was still empty. What would he do when he saw it?

He'd probably throw it into the ocean, and she deserved it.

She rolled the dough just the way David described. Although her technique needed a lot of fine tuning, she could actually see the beginning of a *pain au chocolat*. Once she folded and tightly sealed in the chocolate squares, just like David had instructed, she covered the sweet rolls and placed them in the refrigerator for the night. She couldn't wait to bake them in the morning.

The oven beeped from the other side of the kitchen and she squealed when she pulled out the tray of fourteen éclair pastries. They were all golden brown, just like David's. She jotted down notes about the experience, all the while taking pictures of each step.

If only it were summer, she thought to herself. Then she'd have some really nice shots to take. An outdoor space, the harbor, weddings...

She stilled her pen and looked out the window again. The darkness seemed unbalanced. Her eyes moved to his apartment light. She looked for the bag she had hung on the doorknob.

It was gone.

She dropped the pen and moved to the other set of windows, covering the reflection from the light. Under the streetlights, she saw him. He jogged through the village square to the footbridge, and headed across to Vivi's with the red bag in his hand. She ran to the mirror and checked herself over. She looked at her flannel pajamas, wishing she had time to change, but he had already reached the driveway.

She swung the front door open as he ran up the steps, but he stopped when he saw her. Then, without saying a word, he walked up to her, wrapped his arms around her neck and twined his fingers in her hair. For what felt like a minute, he kept his green sea-glass eyes on her. She could hear her heart pounding in her chest as she just waited. He pulled her in closer and kissed her.

He stumbled her backwards, into the front hall, and held her tightly in his arms. He kicked the front door shut behind him.

CHAPTER 17

*M*att watched as Katie slept in the crook of his arm. She had fallen asleep as they sat by the fire. He didn't move all night. At that moment, he paid attention to the muffled crash of waves, her soft breath, and the morning light sneaking through the windows. He had never been happier.

Every few minutes his heart skipped a beat, looking at her. It wasn't a dream. Katie O'Neil slept right next to him. He wanted to kiss her all over again, but he also wanted to take this all in. He didn't know what the day held. With Katie, it was completely unpredictable.

Suddenly, her arms stretched out as her fingertips wandered out to him. A smile grew across her face as his hands touched hers. Slowly, she opened her eyes.

"Good morning." He leaned forward, and her lips fit perfectly in the crevice of his.

She rubbed his hands and he grimaced.

"What happened to your hand?" she asked, just noticing his swollen knuckles.

Instead of answering, he held her chin and kissed her again, taking in her sweet scent. She sat up, but he pulled her back into the same spot, not wanting her to leave. The night had gone from miserable to magical. They sat in front of the fire with a glass of wine and talked. Then kissed, but mostly talked. He wanted to take things slow. To enjoy the pleasures in front of him, like that very moment.

He was so wrapped up in his head of perfectness, that he almost didn't register the doorbell rang. Katie jerked and sat up on her elbow, listening.

It rang again. Matt looked at the clock. It was barely daybreak. Who'd come to Vivi's this early in the morning?

She looked at him. "Do you think someone's here for you?"

Matt grabbed his phone off the coffee table and checked to see if he had any messages. Nothing. He shook his head, just as confused.

When the doorbell rang a third time, it was like a light went off in her head. She kissed him on the lips as she jumped up off the floor.

"It's Vivi! I forgot to fix the garage door after the power went out." She stood up. "Oh! I cannot have my sweet aunt seeing you wake up here in the morning!"

His jacket hung off the couch, and his boots sat in the hallway.

"Hang out in the bathroom. I'm going to make her some coffee. You can sneak out when we're in the kitchen."

She was about to sweep out of the room, but he grabbed her arm and pulled her into him, kissing her again. "You have to invite me in for breakfast when I ring the doorbell."

"I did make a few pastries last night."

He kissed her once more, then grabbed the things he could find and ran into the bathroom. After he shut the door, he leaned on the bathroom sink and turned on the water.

He looked at himself in the mirror, and thought, *things don't get much better than this.*

∼

Kate practically skipped to the front door. She could hear the bathroom door close behind her and her heart jumped inside her chest. The smile on her face just kept growing.

"Vivi?" she called to the front door. Her heart fluttered again. She was unexpectedly excited to see her aunt.

When she swung the door open, a rush of cold air blew her hair behind her shoulders. Eric faced her from the bottom step. Her mouth went dry. Any words she might have summoned were lodged in her throat.

The silence felt as cold as the air.

His eyes were bloodshot. "I'm so, so sorry."

A sour taste filled her mouth as she studied his face. She couldn't believe it.

Then she remembered Matt in the bathroom.

She looked at Eric. His eyes didn't leave her, and a red puffiness made them droop. He looked like he hadn't slept for days.

He looked absolutely miserable.

"What are you doing here?" It was all she could say.

"I totally freaked out." He looked away, out at the harbor, then back to her. "But I know now, more than anything, that I want to spend the rest of my life with you."

When he finished, he stood there staring at her, his pain palpable.

"I've tried calling you for a couple of days, and when you didn't answer…" He swallowed before he said, "I just needed to hear your voice. To see you again."

She looked out at the driveway and saw his rental car, an upscale SUV, probably with four-wheel-drive, parked next to the minivan. That was her dream sitting in the snow before her. Why did it feel so empty and cold?

His eyes flickered to the side and he made a face. She looked behind her and noticed the wine glasses on the coffee table. He then stepped onto the front stoop, examining. He looked puzzled at first, then surprised, as though he'd been sucker punched. "Is there someone here with you?"

Kate didn't know what else to say but the truth. "Yes."

At that moment, the floorboards creaked from down the hall.

His eyes scanned the space and then said, "Oh my God."

He sat down on the front steps, putting his head between his hands. He began taking deep, heavy breaths. Then he stood, his face bright red.

"Is there another *man* here?"

"Eric."

The cold poured in as she stood with the door open.

He straightened up, blew out a breath and said, "I don't care about anything except you."

Matt tried everything he could not to listen to their conversation. He thought about breakfast. He thought about getting his boat back and going out with Katie, dragging the pots out of the water. He thought about his schedule, towing and making deliveries for Frank and David. He thought about how strange the nickname *john* was for a bathroom. He tried everything he could to not think about how Katie's ex-fiancé stood, but nothing worked.

"You should leave." Katie's voice traveled through the door.

His heart pumped inside his chest as he waited for Eric to respond.

"Please, Kate, we need to talk."

He heard her hesitate. He hated that he was hiding in the bathroom. Worse, he knew Eric was right. They did need to talk, but that didn't mean he wanted her to.

"You don't get to make demands." Her voice held an edge. She was also right. "You can't just come back and expect that a *sorry* will fix things."

"Please, I have to talk to you."

Matt could hear the fear in the guy's voice. He was afraid he'd lost her.

"I needed to talk to you. *You* never called. Why would you expect me to welcome you in?"

"Why, because *he's* here?" Eric's voice grew higher with each word. "You can come out, or you can keep hiding!"

"Eric, please," Katie said. "You need to leave."

He couldn't stay in hiding in the bathroom, and he certainly wasn't going to let this guy be a jerk to her. He opened the door, and Eric saw him right away. He was tall. He stood in a wool pea coat and shoes that probably cost the same as Matt's entire wardrobe. He didn't look like a jerk, like Matt had hoped. He looked like a guy who just lost the love of his life, and Matt instantly felt sorry for him. Because Matt felt the same fear Eric did. He was afraid of losing her, too.

When Matt came closer, he tried to focus only on her, ignoring the fact that Eric now stood in front of the door. "Are you okay?"

She nodded. "I'm fine."

He looked at Eric, then back at Katie. "You two should probably talk."

"Matt, no." She wrapped one arm across her stomach, while her other hand went to her lips. "Please, stay."

"No, you should talk." He forced himself to swallow. He put his coat on and turned toward the kitchen, to go out the garage and bypass the front door, but he stopped in front of her. With his back to Eric, he cupped her elbow in his hand.

Katie stood there, her eyes tearing up. She whispered, "You don't have to go."

He smiled and nodded. "You two really should talk." Matt looked quickly at Eric. A hint of anger now flinted in the man's eyes. He turned back to Katie and recited the speech he prepared in the bathroom. "He doesn't deserve you. I don't even deserve you, because when I was sixteen, I was too stupid to know that letting you go would be the biggest mistake of my life."

He locked eyes with her for a second. He wanted to see if she believed him this time. But her eyes swirled with emotions he couldn't decipher. He squeezed her elbow twice.

She placed her hand on his and squeezed it back, twice.

As he left through the kitchen, Eric stepped further inside and he immediately regretted leaving. What did he just do?

CHAPTER 18

*E*ric sat on the coffee table and put his head between his hands. Kate sat in front of him on the couch.

He looked up. His eyes showed his pain. "I messed everything up, didn't I?"

He seemed so innocent as he said it that Kate almost reached out to grab his hand and pull him closer, but she stuffed her hands under her legs.

Then she studied his face. The last time she saw him was when he told her he couldn't marry her. The look on his face when he said those words had flashed through her mind over and over again throughout the week. It was a look of relief. As though he had confessed a sin. As if a burden had been lifted from his chest.

When he first said it, she was confused. Then he'd said it again. "I can't do this."

She had been at his place, helping him pack for Camden Cove. At first, she'd thought he didn't want to go on vacation because of work. "Please tell me this isn't about the Morrow account. Their money will be there waiting for you when we get back. We've been planning this for months. I promise, we're going to have the best Christmas ever."

He shook his head and dropped the clothes he was packing into the suitcase. "No, I can't go with you. I can't do this." He motioned with his hands, not just to the suitcase, but to the whole room. His face changed from fear to relief. He took a deep breath and said, "I can't marry you."

Kate forgot how to breathe. Panic took over her body. Her hands trembled as she leaned against the bed and tried to focus on his words, in case she had misinterpreted what he said.

"What do you mean?" Her voice was barely a whisper.

He sat on the end of the bed, his back toward her. "I'm just not ready. I thought I was, but I'm not."

Kate didn't remember if she'd said anything or not. She just went into automatic mode. She went back to packing again. She grabbed the clothes laid out on the bed and folded and refolded them before sticking them into the luggage. The flight was in the morning, only a few hours away. She could drive to the airport before she regretted anything.

"Kate, I'm sorry," he said, still looking away from her.

She rested her weight on the suitcase, squeezing the sides, not sure what she was even doing. Don't lose it, she kept repeating in her head as he spoke. Trying not to listen, but hearing every word.

"I don't want to hurt you. You're the last person I want to hurt."

"How long have you felt this way? Is there another woman?"

He shook his head. She couldn't tell if that bothered her more. He just didn't want her.

"I love you, but I'm just—"

She zippered the suitcase so quickly that the sound covered up whatever he was saying. She didn't want to know.

"Kate, don't go." Eric sounded sincere, but he didn't get up from the bed.

She turned and looked at him from the bedroom door. "I'll be at Vivi's."

And that was it.

Her whole life changed.

And now as Eric sat before her, she realized she was no longer *that* Kate. *She* had changed.

She took a deep breath and the air came easier this time. She could feel her heart's pace slow. She studied his gray eyes and saw a new man. One full of regret.

"I'm sorry." He leaned over, placing his hands on her knees. "Please forgive me. I don't care about what happened with you and that guy. I just want you to come back home."

She couldn't believe what was happening. She put her hands on his and took a deep breath. "There will always be a part of me that will love you, but I can't go back. Too much has changed."

His head dropped and he pulled his hands away. He blew out a hard breath. "I will do whatever it takes to fix this."

"It's different now." She wanted something for her hands, to rub or fiddle or use as a focal point. She didn't want to look at him and watch him fall apart.

He stood up and walked to the windows, the furthest spot in the room from her. He looked out at the same view she had for days. She didn't say anything, just waited.

"Is it because of him?" He kept his gaze out the window.

"No." She looked up. "And yes." She took a deep breath. "It's mostly because I'm not the same person I was when I last saw you. I've changed."

He let out a huff. "Yeah, I guess you could say that. You didn't used to sleep with random guys before."

His words stung like a slap in the face. She tried to remind herself how upset he was, but she didn't deserve to be treated as though she had something to apologize for.

"You should leave," she said coldly, standing up.

He held up his hands. "I'm sorry. All I want to do is erase the last week and start again."

She took in a deep breath and listened to the waves.

"Please, Kate, please give me another chance."

She had hoped and prayed and begged for this moment to

come. To have him change his mind, to get her dream life back again, but as she sat there, his hands squeezing hers, she realized that dream had ended.

She didn't want to place blame, because he was only the catalyst for her change, but his one decision changed everything for her.

"Eric, I can't."

And just like that, Kate's life changed again.

～

Matt sat in his apartment and watched the car parked in Katie's driveway. The very fancy foreign SUV he couldn't afford. It had only been about twenty minutes since he left her place, but it felt like forever, just sitting around waiting to see what happened next.

He needed to leave. Go somewhere. Anywhere to get away from the fact that Katie was with her ex-fiancé. The guy who she might still love. The guy who wasn't leaving the house.

What if she went back to him? What would he do then? Worse, what if they stayed in Camden Cove to finish their vacation together?

He swept his keys off the kitchen table when he saw another car pull into the driveway. He couldn't tell who it was, but he guessed it had to be Vivi, if that's who Katie had been expecting that morning.

Just as he was going to leave, Alex Martinez knocked on the door.

"Hey, Alex," Matt said as he opened his door.

"Hey, Matt." Standing in full uniform, Alex's demeanor was flat.

"What's up?" Matt had a feeling he knew. Either it was about the sunken boat, Freddy's threat of going to the police, or with Matt's luck, a whole new problem he wasn't aware of.

"We need to talk."

His head dropped. "I take it that it needs to happen now."

Alex nodded, walking inside his apartment.

"I take it Freddy came for a visit."

"No, but I'm waiting for him to show up." Alex rested his hands on his belt. "I get it, I want to deck the guy, and he didn't even sleep with my wife."

Matt slumped onto his couch, putting his head in between his hands. "I know I need to cool it."

"You don't just need to cool it." Alex let out a deep breath. "You need to stop."

"Have you talked to him about my boat?" He didn't need to remind Alex about the situation, but his anger controlled his rationality.

"You'd know more than me." Alex crossed his arms. "Look, Matt, what I'm trying to tell you is that we all understand the *why*. But for your own sake, stay away from Freddy."

"He was talking about Lauren." Matt gave him a look. Freddy was lucky that Alex hadn't been there. Alex was as protective of Lauren as Matt and Jack. "You'd do the same thing."

"You should've just let Lauren take care of herself. God knows she could."

They both let out a laugh.

"Remember when she hit Tommy Appleton in the nose?" Alex shook his head, laughing again.

"She broke it." Matt smiled, thinking of his little brute of a sister.

"Look, just be careful, because next time, he's going to get an attorney, and I can't help you after that." Alex gave him a serious look.

Matt stood up and shook Alex's hand. "Thanks, man."

He looked out one more time toward Vivi's. The car was still there. Jail might be better than sitting around with his raw heart.

∾

Kate heard a woman's voice from the front hall. "Katie! Eric!"

Kate's eyes shot open as she heard Vivi's voice. Before she could say anything, Vivi walked into the living room. "I'm so glad I got to see you guys before you left!"

Eric looked over at Kate, his eyes blood shot, moistened.

"I thought you were getting in tonight." Kate's throat hurt saying the words.

Vivi unwrapped her scarf, and placed it on the back of the couch. Her eyes flickered to Kate then to Eric, reading the room.

"Um… I was just leaving." Eric stumbled over the words. He had liked her aunt when she came out to visit them in the city. They had talked about music and art of the eighties and nineties.

"Oh." Vivi sounded surprised. She looked at Kate. "Well, don't let me keep you. I'll see you later, then?"

"I'm at the Cliff House," he said and he left.

Vivi said something, as he walked past her, but he kept going, not replying.

Kate's whole being felt stuck, buried in emotions, as she watched Eric leave. Once she heard the door close, Kate rushed over and embraced Vivi. She had never been happier to see her than she was at that moment.

"Katie," Vivi squeezed her, "what just happened?"

Kate didn't say anything, just kept hugging her, holding back her tears until her eyes stung.

"Merry Christmas!" Vivi swayed Kate back and forth. "What have you been up to?" Vivi asked as she pulled away. "I tried opening the garage door, but it wouldn't open."

Kate flung her arms into the air. "Everything's completely a mess!" She fell into the couch, tears sliding down to her chin.

Vivi sat down next to her and put her hand on her knee. "What's going on?"

Kate let it all out, tears falling down her cheeks. "Eric left me, and I got stuck in a ditch, and Matt pulled me out. Then there was no breakfast. And I had to go to a Christmas party with Frank and David. And, I've gained like twenty pounds because of eating so many pastries, and then Matt stayed here last night and Eric came this morning, and he wants to get back together, but now he thinks I slept with Matt."

Vivi sat without moving or even blinking. She finally asked, "What happened to your eyes?"

"See!" Kate got up and started to pace. "I'm a complete mess!"

"Slow down." Vivi stood, taking off her jacket, then took hold of Kate's arms, and made her stop pacing. "Let me make some tea, and we can talk about everything."

Kate leaned into Vivi and hugged her again. "I'd love that."

She followed Vivi into the kitchen and sat down at the table. Vivi had always been the cool aunt. Her mom's younger sister's wild side was legendary in their house. Her mom would frequently roll out a story about her aunt to demonstrate what not to do with her life. "When your aunt was sixteen, she did this" or "she did that".

Kate had always admired how Vivi didn't seem to care, either. No matter what her mom said, Vivi would shrug it off. Questions about when she was going to settle down or when she'd have a family of her own were ignored. She never seemed to get upset. And what her mom never understood was that Vivi was happy. Happier than her mom.

As the kettle ticked on the burner, Vivi sat down and let out a sigh. "Why don't you start from the beginning?"

Kate didn't want to go back to the beginning, because she didn't really know where to begin. Did it happen when he left her? Or was it before that? She didn't really know when it all started.

"Did you know my parents were getting a divorce, the summer I came out alone?" Kate asked her.

Vivi scrunched her eyebrows, as if examining her. She nodded. "Yes."

"Did she know about his affair?"

Vivi didn't answer at first, which made Kate wonder if her aunt would hold loyalty to her mother. Kate had never heard the whole story. After the divorce, her mother never spoke of her father again. Never talked about what happened, besides the fact that her father had a new family. Nothing about their marital problems.

Worse, Kate had never noticed any. Before she came home that summer, she'd thought everything was perfect.

Just like with her and Eric.

And now with Matt.

"Yes," Vivi finally answered, "she knew about the affair. That's why she sent you to me, alone."

"Is this why you never married?" she asked her. "Nothing lasts, so why bother?"

Vivi let out a half laugh. "No, unfortunately, that's not why."

"Then it's our family." Kate studied the coastline, watching as a boat followed the horizon. "We're all cursed."

"We're not cursed." Vivi walked over to her. "We're passionate."

Kate rolled her eyes. "Or crazy."

"That, too." Vivi rubbed Kate's back. "I do believe in love, because I had it once."

Kate remembered that there had been men in Vivi's life. Boyfriends who'd come by and introduce themselves to the family, but never stay around long enough to see again the next summer. "Who was it?"

"His name was Phillip." She smiled the moment she said his name.

"What happened?"

The kettle screamed from the stove. Vivi got up and poured the water, bringing it to the table. Kate dropped two tea bags into mugs.

"Gosh, I haven't thought about Phillip in a while." She folded her hands around the mug. "We were engaged to be married."

"What happened between you two? Why didn't it work out?"

"Well, he was a fisherman, and got caught in a storm, the boat capsized and he drowned."

168

Kate's mouth dropped open. She had never heard the story. "I am so sorry. That's horrible."

Vivi slipped her hands out and patted Kate. "Heartbreak is heartbreak. But being scared is another thing."

"Scared?"

"You mentioned Matt?" Vivi somehow didn't seem surprised. "Do you mean Matt Williams?"

"Yes?"

"I decided to come home because Frank and David gave me a call a few days ago when you arrived, and told me about Eric."

"Did you tell my mom?"

"You didn't?"

Kate shook her head. "She'll just say I told you so."

Vivi shook her head. "She'll be devastated for you."

"I didn't want her to hate him…" Kate looked out the window, down at the slip where Maggie Mae was usually moored. It was still empty. "I just don't know what to do. What if Eric really did just get cold feet? What if he still loves me like he did before? And how are Matt and I ever going to work? Long distance relationships never work. Everything with Eric is planned out. Our house, the wedding, our future."

"You have to follow your heart, as corny as that sounds, it's always right."

Kate rubbed her forehead with both hands. "That's the thing. I don't trust mine."

CHAPTER 19

More than anything, Matt wished Kate had a cellphone. That way he could've just texted her what he wanted to say, send her a quick message, and then she could reply. Easy. Instead, he stood in his apartment staring at her aunt's house like a madman trying to figure out what to do. He could go over there. She and Eric had enough time to talk.

Then, just as Matt convinced himself to leave, Eric came out of the house and got into his car. He sped out of the driveway, practically spinning out and into a snow bank as he reversed. But she didn't leave with him.

She'd stayed.

But she didn't leave, either. As five minutes turned to twenty then to forty-five minutes, he grabbed a pen and paper, scribbled a note, stuck it on the door, and left his apartment. He had to get out of there. He was driving himself crazy.

When he walked into his parents' kitchen, Sarah immediately got into it with him. "You look like you haven't slept in days." She walked up to him and examined his face. "Are those the same clothes you wore last night?"

He leaned over and kissed her on the cheek as she hugged him.

"Good morning," he said flatly. "Can I grab a cup of coffee?"

"Of course." Sarah crossed her arms, inspecting him as he got himself a mug. "I can whip up something to eat, if you want."

"Coffee is fine." He didn't have the stomach for food.

His father sat in the recliner with the dog laying on his feet. "Did you hear anything about the boat?"

With everything that had happened in the last twenty-four hours, he just wanted a break from it all. "Nothing yet."

He noticed that his mother kept checking out his swollen hand. What had his sisters told her about the night before?

She must've decided not to bring anything up because she pushed a plate of sticky buns toward him when he sat down at the counter. "Have something to eat."

He shook his head. "No, thanks."

He rubbed his temples. He couldn't stop thinking about what might be happening with Katie right now.

Sarah stood there, watching him, then as if she couldn't hold back any longer, she cut right to the chase. "Did you get into a fight with Freddy Harrington last night?"

He waited for his mom to keep talking. He was sure his sisters filled her in with all the details. He looked down at his swollen knuckles, his fingers still tender. "Sounds like you already know the answer."

"Did Alex come to your place?" This time she didn't even let him answer. "Did Freddy press charges? Because if he did, your father and I can –"

"Ma, stop," he mumbled. He sunk his face behind his mug of coffee. "He just stopped by, that's all."

"So, what's going on with you and Vivi's niece?" Sarah asked.

Matt set his mug down on the counter and got up. "I think I'm going to head out."

He pulled his coat off the back of the stool and stuffed his arm in the sleeve.

"John, didn't you say you needed help with something in the garage?" Sarah stood on her tippy toes to get his attention.

"Hmm?" John mumbled from his recliner.

She waved at him. "Didn't you say you needed to put that salt into the truck?"

John set the newspaper in his lap, looking confused. Then as if a lightbulb came on, he lifted his finger. "Yes! It'll only take a second."

"Sure." Matt stuffed his other arm in his coat, and followed his father out the backdoor.

"I just need an extra hand loading them into my truck for the restaurant." His father had a stack of bagged salt for the parking lot and sidewalks around the restaurant and his apartment. "So, the women won't stop talking about what's happening between you and the girl in the fancy dress."

"Katie?" Matt didn't think his father ever paid attention to the chatter between his mother and sisters.

"Did I ever tell you about how your mom wanted nothing to do with me for the first year we knew each other?" his father asked.

Matt wished he could interrupt his dad and remind him he already knew the story. It was one of the three his father told when giving advice about girls. Matt and his older brother Jack could recite it in carol.

"Then there was prom, and I asked her, even though she wanted to go with Bobby Cyr, and wanted nothing to do with me." There was no stopping his father once he started telling a story. "She even said no at first, but she changed her mind, probably because Bobby's grandmother died, but she ended up as my date."

Matt sighed. It was usually at a transition when the story went off topic, but this time, John stayed on course.

"She wore this light blue dress, with her hair pulled back. I remember thinking how glad I was that I asked her, even though my chances were slim." John stopped and clicked his tongue and said, "I'm still glad I asked her." Then he dragged a bag of salt past Matt and patted him on the back. "Go for the girl."

And with that last piece of advice, John lifted the bag up and dropped it into the truck. He clearly didn't need help.

Matt pulled his keys out of his pocket. "You good?" He nodded towards the bags.

His father smiled. "You headed out?"

Matt started toward his truck. "There's something I've got to do."

He reversed, peeling out, and hooked a right toward Katie's road. He wanted to get there as fast as he could.

When he pulled into the driveway, only the mystery car sat in the driveway. He ran to the door and rang the bell, hoping he wasn't too late.

He imagined taking Katie into his arms as she answered the door, but it was Vivi who opened it.

"Matthew Williams, it's good to see you." She smiled at him in her door. "How's your grandmother?"

"She's great." Matt looked for signs of Katie. "I'm actually here to see Katie."

Vivi's smile faded. "Oh sweetie, you just missed her."

As if on cue, his phone dinged. He looked and saw a photo sent from his Uncle Frank, with a message. *She's at the docks, in case you're wondering.* The photo was of Katie looking out at the harbor.

He jumped into his truck.

Kate parked in Matt's empty space by the restaurant. She scanned the village for any sign of him. The cedar buildings were still decorated from the holidays, and suddenly Christmas felt so long ago.

Her chances were slim, but she walked straight to the dock. Even with the fog blanketing the water, Kate could see the slip was empty. She walked down to where a few wooden dinghies were moored. Their pastel colors reflected in the icy waters. Oars loosely sat inside their bellies.

She had an urge to take one, to paddle across the harbor, go out to the water and find him. As she looked at the boats bobbing in the water, she thought about what she was doing. Matt wasn't here. She wouldn't be able to say goodbye.

She turned back toward the minivan, her footsteps hollow against the wooden platform. She studied the harbor one last time. Sea smoke rose from the water, twisting up into the air as if the ocean itself was exhaling. It was loose and easy and soft. Then the dock shifted, its surface unsteady, the floating dock dipped into the water, shifting the sea smoke around her.

Matt walked onto the wooden platform.

As he came closer, he smiled and stopped a few yards away from her. All the things she was planning on saying now lost in fear. What if she was wrong? What if she once again didn't see things clearly and it ends up like her and Eric? Or like Matt and his ex-wife? Or her parents?

"Katie, I just –" He stopped and so did her heart, as he stood in silence, as if he were contemplating what to say. Thick snowflakes began fell from the sky, tumbling down around them. Then he asked, "Want to go to Perkins Beach and collect sea glass?"

A laugh escaped as she ran to him, wrapping her arms around his neck and kissed him.

"I would love to."

And she kissed him again.

CHAPTER 20

Kate held the empty box and looked out at her office, thinking about what to pack next.

Rodney swiveled in an office chair. "Come on, O'Neil, it's always been you and me." He stood up and walked toward her. "What am I going to do without you?"

Kate smiled and gave him the hug he was looking for. She would miss him, too. She wouldn't deny how much he had done for her. But it was time.

"You'll be fine." She moved to the bookshelf, hurrying, she had a lot to do before tomorrow. But she stopped what she was doing and said, "Thank you, Rodney, seriously. You gave me a chance to learn here and I appreciate it."

"Good luck, O'Neil." He gave her a nod. "You will do great."

It meant the world he stood behind her. Even though she had nothing to stand behind. She had no official office, no legal paperwork claiming to be a business, no employees, and no income, but she knew with all her heart, she was making the right choice.

When he left, she went back to the books on her shelf and stuffed the box. She wanted to get the day over.

She drove down 94 to Minneapolis, her stomach twisted from

nerves. She would meet her sister and pack up her and Eric's house. The fact they were selling a house they never ended up living in seemed more than satirical.

She waited outside the house in her car, not wanting to go in until Jen came, who promised to help pack up the rest of Kate's belongings.

Her phone rang on the console and her heart dropped when she saw her sister's name. "Please tell me you're close."

"I'm so sorry," Jen began. "I can't make it. I got a call from the school nurse. Gabby's sick."

She sat staring at the front door she had always wanted to paint red, like in New England. Red doors were on almost all New England homes.

She would be fine.

"Oh, Kate," Jen's voice became sympathetic. "You'll be okay, you will."

Was she being selfish if she made her sister feel guilty? She wanted to have someone supportive to help her plow through the house of memories and get the heck out.

"Please don't be mad," Jen said. "When Josh comes home, I'll come right away."

"No, it's okay." Kate tried to feign happiness. "I'll be fine."

"Fine?" Jen could read through her better than anyone.

"Well, I'll survive."

"I swear I'll floor it out there as soon as Josh comes home from work."

"No, it's fine." Kate looked at the mid-century bungalow and said, "It's better if I get it done and over with. I have to go."

Letting out a long slow breath, she popped open her car door, got out, and walked up the front walk to the house. The "for sale" sign had been dug through the snow, even though it was under agreement with a buyer. Now it was up to the banks.

When she entered, more boxes were packed than the day before. Eric had been busy. She didn't want any of the furniture, most the books and any of the other items, really. She wanted very little when all was said or done.

She walked through the living room and noticed how the house had been decorated more to the likening of Eric than of her. The walls painted gray and neutral. The leather couch and chairs masculine with decorative pillows that showed a little of herself.

A piece of art hung in the dining room and made her remember the fight over it. Eric liked still life photography. Black and white photographs of the city, the lakes and of the natural landscape of Minnesota filled the walls. She had wanted color and something that symbolized them, but she gave in, like a watercolor of the city or a colored photo of Lake Superior. They got a black and white print of Ansel Adams framed in black.

The photos of her and Eric were still on the mantle. The weekend they spent in Duluth, the Twins game, and camping up in the Boundary Waters. Looking at the photos was like looking at another's social feed or photo album, foreign and distant.

After two hours, she had gone through the bedroom, then the bathrooms and removed anything that was hers. She realized as she walked through the downstairs, nothing of her remained. And it looked exactly the same.

She checked the time. Eric would be out of work soon and she wanted to avoid him if possible. She hurried as she carried out a box to the car, but when she opened the porch door, his car pulled into the driveway.

She carried on, walking out and straight to her car.

"You need any help?" he asked as soon as he got out.

She looked at the box in her hands. "No, I'm fine."

"I can grab another box for you."

She could feel her panic mode set in. Her breath short, her airway tight, her pulse rushed. But as she looked out at him, his gray eyes now softer, kinder than before, all the worry lifted. Things weren't the same for him, either. "Sure."

He gave a nod and headed inside, bringing the biggest one out to her car. "Were you able to finish packing?"

She nodded. "I got most of it. I guess the rest is yours."

He dropped the box into the back of her car and stood. The silence was deafening. "I can't take all that stuff, Kate."

"Really, I don't want it."

"I guess you are in a rush to get back to the guy." He had broken their unspoken agreement to bring up Matt. "Does he not like decorative items?"

She studied him for a moment, then asked what she had wanted to ask from Christmas. "Why didn't you call me?"

"What?"

"When you broke off our engagement and let me go on our vacation alone, why didn't you call me? Or at least text me back?" She was being rhetorical, so she kept talking. "You didn't call to see if I was okay, or if I made it safely. You didn't call to wish me a Merry Christmas even though you knew I was alone. You didn't text me back when I texted you. Not for at least a few days. Not once. You may have called off the engagement, but your silence ended our relationship."

He placed his hands on his hips and dropped his head. "You're right."

"The worst part was that you made me feel as though there was something wrong with me." Kate blew out a hard breath. "I need to get the last of my things and I'll be on my way."

She walked back to the house and Eric followed behind. No need for further conversation. They both grabbed another big box, carried it out to the car. They worked in silence bringing the rest of her things to her Volkswagen hatchback.

When there was no more room, she still had a few boxes left sitting in the kitchen.

"I can bring the rest to your mother's, if you'd like," he said.

She shook her head. "I'll come and get it."

"You must be starving." He took off his tie. "I was going to order some dinner. Would you like to have something to eat before you go?"

She shook her head. "No. I should get going."

"Let's not make our last moment together like this."

"Like what?"

"Come on, Kate. We loved each other at one time." His eyes were pleading.

She closed the back of her car, twisting the keys in her hands. As she stood there, she felt no animosity toward him. In fact, she felt a strange excitement. A chapter of her life had finally ended.

"Goodbye, Eric." She reached out and gave him a hug. He tried to say something, but she got into the car, not hearing a word.

She smiled as she started the engine. *New beginnings are often disguised as painful endings.*

"Is it necessary for everyone in the family to drive me to the airport?" Matt asked Elizabeth.

Jack rolled his eyes, flipping the keys in his hands. "Are we going or what?"

"Be patient." Elizabeth dropped a tea bag into a mug. "It's a long drive and I want a cup of tea."

"Seriously?" Matt bounced his knee. "If we don't leave soon, I'm going chicken out."

"You won't miss your flight, I promise."

"Make me one then, too," Jack said, stuffing the keys in his pocket.

"Are you kidding me?" Matt grabbed his hockey bag, his make-shift suitcase. "You, two, are killing me"

He walked out the door to the van where inside Frank, David and his mother sat. He slid open the minivan's door, his mother's van. The three of them took the back.

"Where's your brother and sister?" Sarah asked, looking up at the apartment door.

"They're making tea."

"They're making tea upstairs?" Frank shook his head. "They could've just asked for a cup from us."

Matt shrugged, not in the mood to talk to anyone, especially not about something like tea. It didn't matter, he supposed, since he was about to die in less than three hours.

"You will not die," Sarah said, reading his mind.

"We'll see." Matt rubbed his hands together and blew on them. The van still needed to warm up. The winter's temperatures still well below freezing.

Soon, Elizabeth and Jack came down from the apartment, and both sat up front. Just as Jack started the engine, Alex Martinez pulled his police cruiser up to them, and got out waving.

"Hey," Jack rolled down his window. "What's up, man?"

Alex shook Jack's hand, but looked inside the van. "I'm actually here to talk to Matt. Where are you all going?"

"We're taking Matt to the airport," Jack said.

"Have you taken a valium or anything?" Alex had known Matt long enough to know his fear of flying.

"I tried to tell him."

"I'm not taking a dog's prescription of a muscle relaxer."

"Veterinary medicine is just as complicated if not more than the human medical practice."

Matt looked at his watch. If they didn't leave soon, he'd be cutting it close, and there would most likely be traffic at that time of the day.

"We really need to get going," he said. "Can it wait?"

"It won't take long," Alex said. "We can talk right here, if you'd like."

Matt figured the family would hear either way, so he opened the door and just stepped out.

"What do you need to talk about?"

"We arrested two men last night, who we believe sunk your boat."

"Really?" Matt couldn't believe it. "How'd-"

"What did he say?" Frank called out from the back of the van.

Jack leaned forward in the seat practically sitting on Elizabeth to hear through the window. "You caught the guys who sunk Matt's boat?!"

"Who is it?" Elizabeth asked.

"We went through all the surveillance tapes from around town on the night they sank your boat," Alex said." We saw two men walking down the dock toward your boat at two-thirty AM, and came back at about three-fifteen AM," Alex said. "Then, with the footage from the tavern's front door camera, we could identify the two faces inside a vehicle driving down Harbor Lane at three-eighteen AM. We then traced the license plates to a man named Bruce Irving from Dorchester, Massachusetts."

"They're from out of state?" It made little sense. "What did they have to gain from sinking my boat?"

"About five thousand dollars."

"What?"

"We charged Freddy last night for hiring the two men to sink your boat."

"Shut up!" Elizabeth mouth dropped.

"We arrested Freddy and the other men last night."

Matt looked at his watch, hoping he didn't have to go to the station. It was already past seven AM, his flight was in less than three hours and they had at least a forty-minute drive. Once the town of Camden Cove found out Freddy paid two guys from out of state to sink his boat, then got arrested, Matt would never be able to leave.

He reached out and shook Alex's hand. "Thanks for everything, man, but I really got to go."

Alex shook it back, a smile on his face. "Absolutely, it's my job."

Matt opened the van's sliding door and jumped in. "Let's go.'

Elizabeth waved out the window as Alex pulled away.

"I can't believe Freddy got arrested." Frank shook his head.

"Serves him right to do such a foolish thing." David tsked his tongue. "I can't believe he thought he could get away with it."

"Five thousand dollars is a lot of money, if Freddy had asked me, I'd have done it for as little as three," Jack teased.

"Jack!"

"Ha, ha." Matt felt his phone vibrate. A text from Kate.

I can't wait to see you.

Do you think you could wait a couple days?

Why?!

I think I might drive instead.

I'll be here the minute you land.

I love you.

I love you, too.

Matt looked up from his phone, Jack had already reached the highway, headed north.

"I wouldn't want to be Justine," Elizabeth said.

All the troubles of his past seemed so irrelevant, so futile, that he laughed at the whole scenario. "Can you imagine Freddy sitting in jail?"

The van erupted in laughter. Jokes about Freddy's sentence floated around the van throughout the drive. David wiped away tears as he kept coming up with new jokes.

When they finally reached the airport, Jack turned the blinker on for the visitor's parking, but Matt insisted they drop him off at departures. "I don't need you all going in with me."

"We want to make sure you get on the plane, that's all," Sarah said from the back.

"We love you. Call us when you get there," Elizabeth kissed him on the cheek.

He leaned in and hugged the old timers in the back, then grabbed his bag and walked away, without looking back. He had just under two hours to go.

The first thing he needed to do was get to a bathroom,

because he was certain he was about to throw up, because of the flight, because of Freddy, but mostly because his life was about to change forever.

~

Katie waited in the baggage claim. In a matter of minutes, Matt would be landing. She couldn't contain her emotions. One minute, she's giggling with happiness while the next, tears of joy as she thought of him walking down the steps toward her.

She asked him to come to Minnesota and drive with her back to Camden Cove. Vivi had offered the guest room and rent free until she found her own place. She would set up her office there, too. After that, she wasn't sure, which freaked out her mom, but she didn't let her bother her.

Her mom told her she was rushing it, but her sister Jen cheered her independence, and helped her rent the trailer to haul all her stuff.

A text sprung her phone to life. **We landed. See you soon.**

See you soon!

She had packed the trailer the night before. They'd leave as soon as they could after having lunch with the family. Everyone wanted to meet Matt, even her dad. The boy they had heard about for years, but never met.

She and Matt planned to leave for Chicago first thing in the morning, spend a few days there, and then hit Niagara Falls. After that, they would head to Quebec to stay with some of Frank's relatives along with Frank and David who were meeting them there. Once they returned to the states, Kate O'Neil Designs would be open for business.

She watched as all walks of life stepped out of the terminal to the baggage claim. Men, women and children took the escalator or climbed down the stairs as time crept along.

Where was he?

She peeked at her phone, triple checking if he had left a

message. Maybe he stopped for the restroom or forgot something on the plane. She looked up, just as a man walked around the corner with a Red Sox baseball cap covering his eyes, but she knew he was looking for her.

As she stepped away from the wall, he saw her, and his grin grew, making her laugh out loud, catching the stranger's attention that stood next to her. She started to walk, as he moved down the steps toward her, crisscrossing through fellow travelers.

When he arrived at the bottom, they stopped in front of each other, but for only a second before he dropped his bag, reached out, and pulled her lips to his then kissed her.

The stranger's eyes had widened.

"Welcome to Minnesota," she said as soon as they parted.

"Thanks for asking me to come."

CHAPTER 21

*E*very April, as long as Matt could remember, his uncles threw a black-tie event at La Patisserie for the season opener. All the commerce in Camden Cove reopened its doors. It had always been one of the big events everyone in Camden Cove looked forward to. Though, only in Maine are winter boots optional as footwear.

David always baked dozens of desserts and treats. Frank bought plenty of champagne for all the guests, and everyone else supplied the rest.

This year's party was no exception. His uncles outdid themselves once again. A string trio played in the background under Christmas lights, as neighbors and business owners of Camden Cove mingled and ate David's delicacies.

Tonight, those same neighbors seemed mesmerized by the newcomer in the black dress. It didn't take long for them to know the whole story of Katie and Matt. How she had just started her own design firm. Half of the town grabbed a business card about some form of design. Had she done menus? Logos? Branding? Could she design a website like Frank and David's but for an inn?

Throughout the night, his mother and uncles made sure to tell anyone who seemed even slightly interested.

Matt watched from the other side of the room as Katie sat with Vivi and all the other female family members. After Elizabeth and Lauren told another embarrassing story of him as a kid, he decided to grab a glass of champagne. Although, he didn't mind being the subject of ridicule as long as Katie enjoyed herself, and she seemed to be enjoying the stories more than the storytellers. That's all he wanted—for Katie to be happy.

"So, you went for the girl," his dad said, popping a chocolate truffle in his mouth.

Matt nodded, looking out at her. "I went for the girl."

Funny how much can change in a year. Last year, when things were at their worst, he made a resolution. He had never made resolutions, but that year he wanted to forget the past. Never did he imagine that the past was exactly what he needed in the end.

As he looked out, watching Katie with his family, laughing as though they were already family, he knew he was going to do everything he could to keep her in his future.

Kate kept her eye on Matt as he walked up with their coats and handed her scarf to her. "Come on, let's go," he whispered in her ear as he grabbed her hand. Only twenty minutes remained before midnight. "We have to hurry."

Kate laughed, confused but thrilled. "Where are we going?"

"The beach."

"Is this why you made me bring Vivi's boots?" Her stomach twirled as she threw on her coat and followed him out of the bakery. Suddenly, the ocean was the only place in the world she wanted to be.

Matt opened his truck's door and they switched out high heels and leather shoes for boots and snow pants. Matt grabbed a couple blankets from the backseat, then grabbed her hand again, pulled her toward the water.

As they reached the beach, he tugged her toward the sound of the waves. They stopped just at the tip of the wave.

"This is the best spot to see the fireworks," he said, laying out a quilt in soft sand, safe from the tide.

They sat down, and he wrapped another blanket around them as she curled up close to him, feeling his warmth through her coat. He pulled her closer and she nestled into his arms, leaning back into his shoulder.

Waves played a soft melody as they sat looking out into the endless night sky. The moon's reflection twinkled against the water like Christmas lights.

Every part of her body tingled with happiness. She couldn't explain it, but she felt everything that had happened in her life, happened for a reason. That all the heartaches and disappointments led her to this exact place in her journey. And at that moment, she wanted her journey to continue in Camden Cove. Forever.

She watched Matt as he gazed out at the water, but he turned as he noticed her looking.

He leaned over and kissed her gently on the lips.

It was one of the best moments of her life.

Then, she noticed a twinkle from below. Something Matt held in his fingers made her look away from the water.

It was a ring.

"Katie O'Neil, will you marry me?"

A blue sapphire round cut twinkled under the moonlight. Set in a vintage rose gold setting, it was the most beautiful ring she had ever seen.

"Yes!"

He smiled, leaned in again, and they kissed as the fireworks exploded above them.

≈

I hope you enjoyed *The Christmas Cottage by the Cove*! The next book in the series, *The Bakery by the Cove*, focuses on Ally and Michael, two bakers who have their differences at first, but then discover a recipe for love. Click HERE to read *The Bakery by the Cove*.

Then, click HERE for a FREE copy of *The Wedding by the Cove*, which is only available to newsletter subscribers. This novella takes you to Zoe and Ethan's wedding, where new love blossoms between Amelia and Ryan! Besides the free story, newsletter subscribers also receive special offers and updates on new releases.

Click HERE or visit ellenjoyauthor.com for more information about Ellen Joy's other books.

Cliffside Point
Beach Home Beginnings
Seaview Cottage
Sugar Beach Sunsets
Home on the Harbor
Christmas at Cliffside
Lakeside Lighthouse
Seagrass Sunrise
Half Moon Harbor
Seashell Summer
Beach Home Dreams

Camden Cove
The Inn by the Cove
The Farmhouse by the Cove
The Restaurant by the Cove
The Christmas Cottage by the Cove
The Bakery by the Cove

Prairie Valley Sisters
Coming Home to the Valley
Daydreams in the Valley
Starting Over in the Valley
Second Chances in the Valley
New Hopes in the Valley
Feeling Blessed in the Valley

Beach Rose Harbor
Beach Rose Secrets

ACKNOWLEDGMENTS

There are so many people I'd like to thank for helping with the writing of this book.

First, I'd like to thank my three men. I wouldn't have followed my dreams if I didn't have you all by my side. Thank you for your encouragement, patience and faith in me.

Thank you to my mom, dad, and sister who always believed in me.

Thank you to Katie Page, my editor. A thank you just doesn't feel appropriate enough for what you have done for me and my career. You truly are an angel. Thank you, thank you, thank you.

Thank you to Zoe Book Designs for my beautiful covers!

Thank you to Danielle St. Laurent-Thorne. The best beta reader a writer could ask for! Thank you for your honest feedback, your reader's knowledge and advice. Thank you. I love having you as my friend!

To Darcy Favorite-Brewster, my beautiful cousin and one of my very first readers. Thank you for reading and encouraging me. I'm so lucky to have you as my cousin, but even luckier that you're my friend! Thank you.

Thank you to Debbie Love, my critique partner, for our writing group the Pen Hens. I wouldn't have finished the final draft of my first story if it wasn't for you. Not to mention all the other crazy things you do for me and my family. Your heart is pure gold. Thank you.

Thank you Darlene Phelps-Foss. Thank you for your early edits. You took on a huge project out of the kindness of your heart. I love our sweet town because of people as kind and generous as you.

Thank you to Dr. Robyn Eldredge, the real Dr. Elizabeth, for being my friend and always inspiring me. Thank you for reading my early versions and being my first fan.

Thank you to Tina Durham-Bars who is always up for proofreading.

Thank you to Teresa Malouf for proofreading as well!

Thank you to my local chapter of Romance Writers of America in New Hampshire. You ladies are totally inspiring and I want to be like all of you someday.

Thank you to all the readers who picked up this book. I hope you enjoyed it as much as I did writing it. I'd love to hear from you, please join my newsletter and reach out to me by going to my website!

www.ellenjoyauthor.com

ABOUT THE AUTHOR

Ellen lives in a small town in New England, between the Atlantic Ocean and the White Mountains. She lives with her husband, two sons, and one very spoiled puppy princess.

Ellen writes in the early morning hours before her family wakes up. When she's not writing, you can find her spending time with her family, gardening, or headed to the beach. She loves summer and flip-flops, running on a dirt country road, and a sweet love song.

All of her stories are clean romances where families are close, neighbors are nosy, and the couples are destined for each other.